THE GO

Teresa Waugh has translated
numerous books from French and Italian.
The Gossips is her sixth novel.
She lives in Somerset.

Teresa Waugh

THE GOSSIPS

Mandarin

A Mandarin Paperback
THE GOSSIPS

First published in Great Britain 1995
by Sinclair-Stevenson
This edition published 1996
by Mandarin Paperbacks
an imprint of Reed International Books Ltd
Michelin House, 81 Fulham Road, London SW3 6RB
and Auckland, Melbourne, Singapore and Toronto

A CIP catalogue record for this title
is available from the British Library
ISBN 0 7493 9547 8

Printed and bound in Great Britain by
BPC Paperbacks Ltd
a member of
The British Printing Company Ltd

For my granddaughters,
Constance, Beatrice, Mary,
Esther and Sally

I

'She's sure to have some kind of breakdown.'

'Oh, Camilla, do you really think so?'

'I'd be quite surprised if she didn't – she's very tense at the best of times, so I don't see how she can possibly cope with all this. You know the police were round there yesterday – all afternoon?'

'Gosh! Were they really? Who told you?'

'Isabel. She saw them arriving. She'd just come back from Sainsbury's. Well, she said she'd been to Sainsbury's – who knows what she was really doing . . .'

'Oh you are awful! Of course she was at Sainsbury's if she says so.'

'I'm not so sure. I know she went there on Monday, and nobody in their right mind goes there more than once a week – and – didn't you know? People are saying that Isabel's having an affair with Walter.'

'She can't be. He's peculiar and, anyway, Sarah thinks he must be gay.'

'Hey, do you think he really is? I never thought of that, but I must say it explains a lot. So, if it's not Walter, who do you think Isabel is having an affair with?'

'I've no idea, but I'll tell you if I find out. But what's this about Annie and the police? That's awful – and what if she does have a breakdown? What'll she do? Who'll look after Tamsin?'

'I suppose she'll have to go to her father . . .'

'She can hardly do that if he's been abusing her . . .'

'Shsh – Fanny – do be careful what you say. We don't know . . . But I doubt that the poor girl has a very nice time anyway. Annie's never liked her you know. Imagine not liking your own child!'

'I know. It's terrible, but she never was at all maternal.'

'I don't know why people like that have children in the first place.'

'It was probably an accident. She'd had so many abortions she just couldn't face having another.'

'Look, I think I'd better go now; this telephone bill's going to be enormous – and it's the expensive hour.'

'I'll give you a ring tomorrow if I hear any more. Lots of love – 'bye.'

'Lots of love – 'bye. . . .'

Annie was alone at last. All alone with her Christmas tree, that is to say. She looked at it standing forlornly in the corner of the sitting-room where it had begun to shed its needles on the carpet. It looked dusty now, and desiccated as though it had a will of its own and longed to be dismantled. It was funny, Annie thought, how a tree which before Christmas had been such an emblem of good cheer, gaudily announcing the festive season, could so soon become a sad thing of the past, almost hanging its head in shame as one colourless January day succeeded another.

She was tired and she was glad that the house was empty. Dreadfully tired. She had no desire to do anything about the wretched Christmas tree and she didn't want the bother of hoovering the pine needles off the carpet, but neither did she want to see it there as a dreary reminder of the time of year and of the two bleak months to come. She looked at her watch which told her that it was January 7. The tree should have come down yesterday and she could have asked Tamsin to do it then, but Tamsin, in her present mood, would probably have refused.

Yes, Tamsin would probably have refused, which was peculiar and Annie's fault, perhaps. Annie knew that at the age of fifteen she would never have dared to refuse to do anything which her mother had told her to do. Sometimes, even now, she found it difficult to disobey her. She gave the tree another long look and finally decided to turn her back on it for the moment. She wanted a drink, which she decided to take to her bedroom where she need no longer look at the tree which could wait until the morning.

It was supposed to be unlucky to leave your tree up after Twelfth Night. Annie smiled wryly to herself. She didn't know about bad luck but she'd certainly had enough trouble last year, what with Tamsin and having to leave her job. She wondered what on earth might be waiting around the corner this year.

She went upstairs, lay on the bed and flicked on the remote-control button of the television. In the small house, her bedroom was her favourite room and the only place where she could ever feel totally relaxed and protected from the outside world. It was a warm, dark-red, untidy room but, as the house faced south, when the sun shone it was filled with dancing light which glanced off the oval gilt frame of a pale pastel of her granny in a blue dress and made patterns on the wall as it played on the sides of the two glass pyramids given her by Will. She could spend hours gazing at those pyramids, engrossed by the patterns made by the sun, but now, late on a January

3

afternoon, the room was almost in complete darkness. A dull darkness which coincided with Annie's mood, and she liked it. Beside her on the bedside table there was a bottle of white wine and hanging on a knob of the brass bedstead was Will's dressing-gown. Gathering dust, she thought. She must try to drink no more than just two glasses of the wine.

Three quarters of an hour later Annie was still on her bed and the bottle, she noticed as she refilled her glass, was two-thirds empty. She had been thinking about Tamsin and hadn't realised how much she was drinking.

Tamsin had gone to stay with her father for the weekend, which was just as well, Annie supposed, although she had strangely little insight into what Tamsin really thought or felt about Henry. She did know, though, that Henry and Henry's new wife dreaded the arrival of Tamsin over whom they had absolutely no control and who upset the easy tenor of their cosy life and the easy tenor of their cosy new baby. Annie didn't blame anybody. She merely acknowledged to herself that life was a mess, and occasionally wondered what she was doing, bothering to lead it.

Annie sometimes thought that she might have spoilt Tamsin, her adored, long-awaited child. There had been a couple of miscarriages and then a child had died inside her at six months. It had been horrible and she had been warned not to try again. So, of course, when Tamsin finally arrived, she had been greeted like a small miracle. Annie had always wanted children and from the very first she had doted on Tamsin, imagining her, at every stage of her advancement, to be exceptionally gifted, exceptionally beautiful and exceptionally athletic. At one point she became almost embarrassed for the mothers of less talented children, believing them all to be envious of her perfect darling. In fact Annie was so embarrassed that she

4

took to denigrating her own child in public for fear of rubbing the other mothers' noses in the inferiority of their own children. This became something of a habit so that by the time Tamsin was fifteen her permanent cry was that her mother had ruined her life by undermining and belittling her.

In fact Annie still believed that the disordered adolescent was potentially a star. Annie adored her and lived and breathed in fear for her, for she never knew what Tamsin would think of doing next and only knew, with a nagging dread, that it would probably be something foolish and even dangerous.

Christmas hadn't in fact been too bad; Tamsin had held her horses even to the point of being vaguely polite to her grandmother. It wasn't so much the shopping and the cooking which exhausted Annie at Christmas as the orchestrating of the family. The trying to see that her mother was not riled, that Tamsin trod on no one's toes, that her brother kept his right-wing opinions to himself and that her sister didn't cry. It was her destiny to be responsible for them all at that time of year and they all always lunched with her in Notting Hill.

Annie's house, tucked away in Hillgate Village, behind Notting Hill tube station, was in a quiet street of brightly painted, early nineteenth-century workmen's cottages, a bit jerry-built, but somehow resistant to the passage of time despite insidious rising damp and somewhat insecure foundations. Sometimes, when she walked down her street, it reminded her of nothing so much as the set for a musical comedy. Whenever a house changed hands, it was always a matter of concern what colour the newcomers would paint it. There were a few nasty years when number fourteen, on which Annie looked out, was painted a hideous shade of purple, but it had lately been changed to a more tasteful mushroom with an olive-green

5

door. Annie's house was always painted grey and her door was always white, but, whilst never wishing to choose them for herself, she rejoiced in the cheerful blues and pinks and yellows of her neighbours.

Upstairs there were two small bedrooms – Annie's and Tamsin's – with a bathroom on the half-landing. The sitting-room was on the ground floor – a typical London sitting-room, long and thin – and behind that there was a cloakroom. The kitchen took up most of the basement, but there was a poky little room at the back which might have been used as a dining-room, but where Annie preferred to have her desk and some filing cabinets. The house was quite big enough for her and she loved it. Indeed, it seemed to represent the one constant in her life since the time of the break-up of her marriage some five years earlier.

Suddenly the doorbell rang. Annie glanced at her watch and wondered who it could be. She wasn't expecting anyone as far as she could remember. As she got off the bed she felt decidedly drunk and it seemed to take her ages to put her shoes on, which was hardly surprising as she began by spending some time pushing the left shoe round with her right foot and vice versa. She didn't want to go to the door shoeless. She had done that yesterday and felt rather foolish as a result.

Tamsin had been out and Annie had sat down for a moment to read the paper just after lunch with her shoes kicked off, when the bell had rung. She'd opened the door to find two policemen on the doorstep, which had immediately made her heart leap into her mouth as she wondered where Tamsin was and what she had done now. Then she realised, to her amazement, that one of the policemen was holding a beautiful blue Persian cat in his arms.

The cat she recognised as coming from a house three

doors down – the lemon-yellow one – and so had directed the policemen to take it there.

'He nearly lost one of his nine lives just now under the wheels of a van,' said one policeman. 'Sorry to trouble you, Miss,' he added as she closed the door.

'Miss,' she thought, must have been in deference to her bare feet.

As she finally got the right foot into the right shoe, Annie heard the bell ringing again rather impatiently, and then as she came downstairs she heard the letter-box clattering and a voice calling, 'Anyone at home?'

It was Sarah. Annie thought she needn't have bothered about her shoes for Sarah's sake. Or perhaps it was just as well that she had because Sarah had a funny way of looking at one and at times an even funnier way of interpreting what she saw.

'Hi,' said Sarah, as Annie opened the door. 'Are you busy?'

'Not at all, come on in.'

'I don't want to be a bore,' said Sarah, 'but I was just passing so I thought I might as well bring you back this.' She held out an earthenware terrine which Annie had lent her before Christmas.

Sarah was an old friend of Annie's but Annie was never really sure that she could entirely trust her. There was sometimes something a bit disingenuous about her. For instance, Sarah could hardly have happened to be passing by with an earthenware terrine; in fact she must have taken the terrine out with her with the express purpose of bringing it back to Annie. Annie wondered what Sarah really wanted. She looked at her watch.

'It's not quite six,' she said, 'but what about a drink? Or would you prefer a cup of tea?'

'A gin and tonic would be fine,' said Sarah as she sank into the sofa. She looked round the room. Annie, she always thought, had rather old-fashioned taste but her house never failed to look warm and welcoming. There were bookshelves on either side of a pretty Victorian marble fireplace, and the walls, which were papered in green-and-white stripes, were hung with rather smudgy oil paintings of country churches and villages and cows and sheep, all picked up by Annie for a song at sales and in the odd second-hand shop. The room was filled with ornaments of every kind. Pretty and monstrous, old and new, they came from junk shops or had been brought back from all the corners of the earth by Annie or Will. The chairs and sofa were comfortable and shabby. A Christmas tree was crammed into a corner of the room. It leaned at an awkward angle and, Sarah thought, looked rather forlorn. It ought to have been taken down by now.

'Still got your tree up, I see,' she said. 'I took ours down days ago, I couldn't stand the sight of it any longer. Where's Tamsin?'

'Gone to Henry's for the weekend.' Annie poured a gin and tonic for Sarah and then a small glass of whisky for herself. She would have to go carefully. She wondered what time it was when she had opened the bottle of wine.

Sarah looked at Annie sitting opposite her with her shoes kicked off. Annie was dark. Now she looked thin and pale and sad.

'How are things?' Sarah asked, in a meaningful and, Annie thought, somewhat intrusive way.

'Fine,' said Annie. She didn't feel like talking to Sarah at the moment.

'You just look rather done in,' Sarah said. 'I hope you're okay.'

'Everyone's done in after Christmas. Look at the weather and look at that bloody tree.' She wished Sarah hadn't seen, let alone mentioned, the tree. 'There hasn't been a ray of light for days.'

There was a pause. Annie sipped her whisky, determined to say nothing.

'Heard anything from Will?' Sarah enquired after a moment.

Annie ignored the question. She was beginning to feel rather annoyed. What right did Sarah have to come barging in talking about terrines and trying to find things out when Annie had been quite happy, alone for a moment, getting quietly drunk in the privacy of her own bedroom?

Sarah was getting nowhere. She decided to try another tack. 'Did I see the police round here yesterday?'

'Police? Or course not.' Annie had genuinely forgotten for the moment about the two policemen with the Persian cat on the front doorstep.

'Funny,' said Sarah, 'I thought I saw them here as I passed.'

'Oh, the police – yes, I forgot, of course,' Annie said as the memory of them suddenly dawned on her. But she was not prepared to put Sarah out of her agony, so she said no more, but changed the subject completely. 'How're the boys?' she asked.

'I'll be glad to get them back to school,' Sarah said with a twinge of bitterness. 'It's a full-time job keeping them out of trouble in the holidays. Neil's taken them skating this evening.'

Sarah's two boys were spoilt little monsters in Annie's opinion, and as far as she could see it was just as well that they went away to a smart boarding-school in the Home Counties, although she knew that, when they had first gone, Sarah had wept bitter tears. Sarah's husband Neil not unnaturally insisted that his sons should be properly educated, as he had been. Of course, if they had been girls, it would have been different. Once the decision was final and Sarah had wept her bitter tears, there was no

9

alternative for her but to pretend that what was happening was just what she had wanted from the start. From that time onwards Annie had observed her friend hardening almost visibly towards the boys.

Deprived of her babies, Annie thought, as she glanced at her friend. Sarah seemed to have changed so much since the carefree days of their youth – but then so, no doubt, had she. But, in Sarah's case, there was an undeniable bitterness, as if she felt that she had been cheated somewhere along the way. She looked young for her forty-three years, and was as pretty as ever – small and neat and blonde.

'I don't know if I ought to tell you,' Sarah began in a hesitant voice as she twisted her glass in her hand and looked down at it thoughtfully with her head on one side. Her pretty little head. 'Well, if it was the other way round, I'm sure I'd want *you* to tell *me* . . .' A light, insincere tone which Annie knew well had crept into Sarah's voice.

Annie looked at her glass which was empty and wondered if she dared have any more whisky. She wanted it but she knew that she was drunk enough already and besides she couldn't really be bothered to get out of her chair. She waited quietly to hear what Sarah was going to say next.

'You know I don't like gossip,' Sarah went on in the same light tone, 'in fact, I denied it all of course – but I still think you ought to know that everybody's saying that you're having a nervous breakdown because of Henry having abused Tamsin – I mean, isn't it awful? How can people say such horrible things?'

In Annie's opinion, Henry had a lot of faults, starting with priggishness and going on to hypocrisy, but she was certain that he was not a child abuser. She said nothing: she didn't want to allow herself to get angry. Instead she thought about Will and wondered if he was safe.

'It must have been awful having the police round here for half the afternoon yesterday – for all anybody knows, they were here about a parking fine, but Isabel's told everyone she saw them and you can imagine what's being said now . . .'

Funny, Annie thought, that Isabel and Sarah should both have chanced to see the two policemen during the few minutes they had been at her front door. Isabel lived in the road which formed a 'T' with the bottom of Annie's street, and she was very likely to come down it in order to get out into the Bayswater Road, but Sarah lived in the next-door parallel street and could have no possible reason for passing on her way anywhere.

Annie said, 'I hope they're all enjoying themselves gossiping. Personally, I couldn't care less what they're saying. They'll soon get bored and then they'll have to find someone else to talk about.'

'I don't know how you can take it so calmly,' said Sarah. 'I don't think I could bear it – but then there's been nothing for anyone to say about me for years.'

'I wouldn't be so sure,' Annie said. She didn't add that more than one of their friends had taken a certain pleasure in confiding in her surreptitiously that Sarah had always been in love with Will. So much so, in fact, that it was widely believed that Sarah had only persuaded Neil to move to Hillgate Village so that she could be near Will when he was in England. She had certainly taken tremendous care at the time to point out endlessly to everyone what an advantage it was going to be living so near Annie – her oldest and dearest friend, Annie.

Sarah looked momentarily embarrassed and gave a little, short, artificial laugh. 'Well, as long as you're all right,' she said, 'and I can deny that any of it is true, then I'll feel much happier.'

'Why do you bother to listen to gossip about your friends?' Annie wondered.

It was Sarah's turn to pretend not to have heard. 'Well, I'd better be getting on,' she said, 'or the children will be home before me. Thanks for the drink.'

I'm glad, Annie thought as she kissed her friend goodbye, that I haven't got your horrid little turned-up nose, poking it into everyone else's business.

'I'll give you a ring when I've got rid of the boys,' Sarah said, 'and we'll have lunch.'

When Sarah had gone, Annie went back to bed and turned on the television again. She was feeling slightly sick, so managed to resist the temptation to refill her glass. Sarah had completely spoilt the peaceful, quiet time she had been relishing on her own. What a bitch Sarah, whom she'd always thought of as a friend, was turning into. What was the matter with her? And what was her hidden agenda? Perhaps she really was still in love with Will. Everyone knew they'd had a fling years ago – but years ago. Before Sarah was married and before the boys were born – and the older one must be eleven by now. Annie didn't feel remotely threatened by Sarah as far as Will was concerned since Will always said – and she supposed he was telling the truth – that Sarah spelt trouble. She became tricky once you were closely involved with her. Annie knew what Will meant and decided to steer clear of Sarah for a while.

There was nothing worth watching on the television so Annie fell asleep. When she awoke, she felt cold and the telephone was ringing; the television was still jabbering at her. She took a minute or two to realise what was happening and to fumble for the telephone.

It was Will! Will in Sarajevo. She hadn't heard from him since before Christmas.

'Fanny, it's Sarah. Hi! How're you?'

'Fine. 'nd you?'

'Fine. I had to ring because I felt I must talk to somebody; I've just been round to see Annie.'

'How was she?'

'I'm really worried about her. I think she's probably about to crack up. Poor Annie, it's too awful.'

'Why? What's happened?'

'Well, she looks awful – and she was drunk at three o'clock in the afternoon. And, do you know, she hadn't even taken her Christmas tree down . . .'

'Really? Poor Annie. Is there anything anyone can do for her?'

'What can be done? I mean, if she won't even talk to me – and I'm her oldest friend . . . I've known Annie since we were both sixteen, you know. She was so pretty when she was young . . .'

'She still is . . .'

'No, Fanny, honestly, not if you'd seen her this afternoon. She looks a hundred years old, and drawn, and thin, and pale. She looks dreadful. Mind you, it's not surprising. She hasn't even heard from Will for God knows how long. I always doubted that that relationship could last. Will's too romantic for Annie really – I never thought it would work.'

'When did she last hear from him, then?'

'Well, she didn't say exactly – but not for ages, that much is obvious.'

'Did she say anything about Tamsin?'

'Only that she'd gone to stay with Henry for the weekend – and then she looked – well sort of – I can't quite explain. I'm sure there's something nasty going on there. And the police were round there all yesterday afternoon . . .'

'Gosh! What happened?'

'Well, it obviously wasn't too good. She looked pretty shattered when I mentioned it. She didn't really want to go into it, though.'

'I'm not surprised. I always thought Henry was a creep, didn't you?'

'Yes, but who on earth would have imagined that? And God only knows what's going to happen next. But I'll be in touch with Annie. I'll ring her or call round every day while things are bad.'

'Let me know if there's anything I can do.'

'I don't really think there's anything any of us can do . . . It wouldn't be so bad if Will could be relied upon in any sort of way, but there it is . . .'

'He can't help; he's never here. And, by the way, have you heard about Isabel? She's having an affair with Walter.'

'Is she really? Who told you that?'

'Oh – everyone knows . . .'

'Hallo.'

'Hallo, Camilla. It's Fanny.'

'How are you?'

'I've just been talking to Sarah – and, by the way, she never said anything about Walter being gay.'

'Well, perhaps he isn't. I dunno. She told me he was.'

'You know, she's a bit of a cow, Sarah.'

'Oh, I know she is, but why do you say so in particular now?'

'Well, she's been to see Annie who's supposed to be her oldest friend and all she can do is bitch about her. I think she's really jealous of Annie – and always has been.'

'She's bound to be jealous because of Will, isn't she? He treated her like dirt and I don't think she's ever got over him.'

'I'm sure you're right. In fact I think she'd go off with him now at the drop of a hat, if she had half the chance – leave Neil and the boys – everything.'

'I'm sure she would. But the trouble is she's got so dreadfully bitter, which isn't really surprising – after all Neil's such a pompous old bore and the boys are always away at school. She's got nothing to do, sitting there in that house all day, but wait for her next aerobics class and fantasise about Will and what might have been.'

'I know. Poor thing.'

'But what did she say about Annie?'

'Oh, Annie – she's in a terrible way . . .'

II

'... and Fanny, by the way, what about Tamsin? Has anyone seen her at all?'

'No – I think Sarah said she'd gone to stay with Henry. I say, Camilla – do you really think it's true? It does seem so peculiar when you think of Henry and all that religious stuff.'

'I don't see why it shouldn't be. After all, it's quite wrong, you know, to assume that these things are entirely confined to the working classes. Even in the best homes ...'

'Oh I know all that, but still – well, isn't it just awful? I mean, think of that poor child. Her life will have been ruined. I really can't bear it for her.'

'I know, poor thing, but I believe that she is showing all the signs. What I simply can't understand, though, is why on earth Annie's letting her go and stay with Henry now that all this has come to light.'

'I know, it's extraordinary. Do you ever see Henry these days?'

'I haven't seen him for ages – certainly not since he got married again – and, if I do bump into him, I honestly don't think I'll be able to look him in the eye.'

'I rather agree – not if he's done that.'

'To tell you the truth, I always thought there was something rather odd about Henry.'

'Oh, I don't know. I just thought he was a bit dull – perfectly nice, but just a bit dull.'

'Do you think so? I thought of him as a typical buttoned-up English public schoolboy – and Catholic schools are far worse you know. They teach them to feel guilty all the time and to lie.'

'I don't believe they really teach them to lie . . .'

'Of course they do – all that confession and stuff. They just have to say they're not going to do it again, even if they are, and then they get forgiven. And if they don't go to confession once a week, they're beaten.'

'I wonder if that's really true.'

'I'm sure it is. Why shouldn't it be? It would certainly explain Henry's behaviour, don't you see?'

'You can't pretend that all child abusers come out of Catholic public schools.'

'Of course I never suggested anything of the sort – but those schools are certainly responsible for an awful lot of problems.'

'I can't help it, I don't really believe that about Henry. I mean, why would he do it? He's had two very pretty wives.'

'I don't think that's got anything to do with it. What sex is his new baby, by the way?'

'It's another girl, I think.'

'As a matter of fact, I heard that it might not even be his . . .'

Tamsin found living with her mother claustrophobic. She had begun to feel intensely irritated by almost everything about Annie, and she longed for her mother to stop loving her so much. Anyway, Annie called it love whenever she fussed and bothered over her daughter and she called it love when she worried about her at every moment of the day. Tamsin described it differently. She thought her mother had problems – that she was jealous of the good time Tamsin was having and of Tamsin's social life. She thought Annie lived vicariously through her daughter because her own life couldn't be much fun with Will always away, and with that ghastly set of friends she had. In Tamsin's opinion, Annie ought just to get rid of Will. He obviously wasn't doing her any good, and go and find someone else. Her mother could still be quite decent looking if she tried, and if that Isabel woman who looked years older than Annie could find a string of lovers, which people said she did, why couldn't Annie?

It annoyed Tamsin very much that her mother didn't go out more often. It wasn't fair on Tamsin – she never had the house to herself. She also thought that her mother ought to be more generous with things like money. Annie didn't seem to realise that she was keeping Tamsin in a prison at the one time in her life when what she really needed was freedom. Tamsin's desperate search for freedom had led her into some difficult situations already, but she didn't care, she would go on fighting for her rights and questioning the petty tyranny and the domination until her mother realised that Tamsin was grown-up now and could do what she wanted. She thought of Annie's tired, caring face and of all her 'are you all right darlings?' and she felt she wanted to explode. And why couldn't she have collected Tamsin's things from the cleaners? It wouldn't have hurt her. She didn't have anything else to do. Tamsin thought her mother was really selfish. No wonder if even a visit to Henry's presented itself as a form of escape.

As for Henry, Tamsin was pretty cross with him, too. He'd left them apparently without turning a hair, despite all his Catholic piety, and now he'd got a horrid new little baby. Tamsin had decided from the start to ignore the baby and this she did to the point of denying its existence whenever the occasion presented itself. She sensed that Henry and his wife were both made to feel awkward by her presence, but she didn't care. Her father, she supposed, would have preferred her not to exist. She must be a constant reminder to him of all the lies he had had to tell to get an annulment. Annie he could have put more conveniently behind him – but not Tamsin. She wouldn't allow him to do that – ever.

So Tamsin went to see her father not only to escape the claustrophobia of Hillgate Village, but with the express purpose of reminding him of her existence and of how badly he had behaved. She didn't feel like allowing him to get away too easily with everything he had done. In some corner of her mind she also felt that if she saw Henry it served her mother right for being so bloody forgiving and tolerant. She had never heard Annie utter one word of complaint against him.

Tamsin sat by the window in the train, staring out at the colourless landscape as it sped by. It had snowed a little at the beginning of the week and here and there a few grubby patches remained, pierced by clumps of dead grass. Daylight was beginning to fade and although it wasn't yet four o'clock, lights already shone from windows as they passed. It was a dreary time to be going to the country, but at least Tamsin felt she would have more space in her father's house than at home. She looked at her watch. Another half-hour before the train was due to arrive at Pewsey, where Henry would presumably be waiting uncomfortably on the platform. Tamsin relished the thought of his discomfort for how dared he behave the way he had? How dared he?

Henry had left home five years earlier when Tamsin

was only ten, but she had not yet accustomed herself to the situation, and felt that as one miserable event succeeded another, she never would.

First there had been their home that they had had to leave – a beautiful large house in Islington with a lovely garden – wild for London and full of trees. For some reason which Tamsin had never grasped but for which she would always blame Henry, the dog had had to be put down at the same time. Annie swore that it was riddled with cancer and blind, but Tamsin was never sure that she could believe that. Then Annie and Tamsin had lived in a horrible flat for a while until the new house could be bought. Something to do with money and lawyers. And all the time Tamsin longed for the old house in Islington, and still it was her ideal though changed and romanticised by memory and dreams. She often dreamed that she was back there now.

Henry then moved to Wiltshire – to a Queen Anne rectory, tucked away beneath the Marlborough Downs. He moved there with Angie, his new wife, but they weren't married then although, as Tamsin later discovered, Angie had been pregnant. Angie lost the baby and Henry and she went on living together in their perfect rectory. They slept in separate bedrooms because Henry and Annie weren't divorced yet and – more importantly – Henry hadn't got his annulment, and they pretended to Tamsin and anyone else who was foolish enough to listen that they were just good friends. Sometimes their good friendship must have got a bit out of hand because Angie's little sister, who was older than Tamsin and sharp and spiteful and wanted to be a nun, poked Tamsin in the ribs during mass and whispered in her ear that she knew why Angie and Henry weren't taking communion and she'd tell Tamsin later.

Then there had been all the fuss over the annulment

20

about which Annie hadn't wanted to talk to Tamsin; but Henry, full of piety, was determined to explain it all as clearly as he could. After all, what is the point of an annulment if not to tell the world that you are doing no wrong. God, if He existed, Tamsin thought, would know already. Henry's explanation seemed to her like the description of a view attempted in a fog.

He explained very carefully that her parents' marriage had never in fact been a marriage at all on account of two rather significant facts. One was that there was a question of Annie's mental stability at the time of the wedding. She had been recovering from a broken engagement to a man who had walked out on her at the last minute, when she agreed to marry Henry. One had to ask oneself under the circumstances, whether, at this point, she was in any fit state to make such a momentous decision or to make her marriage vows with the proper intent. The balance of her mind had clearly been disturbed at the time. Having observed the grown-up world around her, Tamsin frankly wondered if anyone was ever in a suitable state of mind to make such promises and really to know what they entailed. When she was thirteen she would have given everything she had to marry Michael Jackson and she could already see that that would have been an appalling mistake, but she would have meant it at the time. No doubt grown-ups were equally capable of such folly. She couldn't see why they had to lie about it afterwards, and anyway, in this instance she took it as a personal insult.

The second and ultimately most important fact, since it was the one whereby Henry gained freedom, absolution or whatever – in effect the right to make love to Angie with a clear conscience – was merely a practical one. By some peculiar chance oversight, it turned out that the banns of marriage had never been properly read three times, thus invalidating the whole procedure. Never mind that marriage, as Tamsin had been carefully instructed, was a sacrament administered by the spouses with the Church as a mere witness. Henry had his answer ready: the witness on this occasion had been incompetent, so of course there could have been no marriage. Tamsin, who was by no means stupid, asked her father if he truly believed that the tree in the quad ceased to exist when he was no longer looking at it.

Henry had pretended not to hear that.

After the annulment came all the rejoicing and, after the banns had been properly read, the wedding, which Tamsin had been made to attend because Angie and Henry had seen fit to wish to include her in this insult to her mother. And they looked into each other's eyes and knew that God had at last licensed their lust and that from now onwards they could share the master bedroom in their perfect rectory.

And now there was this horrid baby.

The train was just coming into Pewsey, seven minutes late. Tamsin decided to get out at the last possible moment to see if she could worry her father. Would he care if he thought she had missed the train, or just wasn't coming? She supposed he would probably be rather relieved and suddenly she wanted to cry. She looked out of the window as the train slid into the station and there was Henry standing awkwardly on the platform, looking anxiously at the lighted windows as the carriages flashed past. He was tall and good-looking, with thick, dark, sleek hair and Tamsin was proud to have a father who looked like that. She thought he was very attractive.

On the way back to the rectory in the car, Tamsin answered her father's enquiries about Christmas in monosyllables. It had begun to rain and she stared sulkily at the rain lashing the windscreen.

'Beastly weather,' said Henry.

Tamsin didn't answer.

'You'll see a big change in Matthew.' Henry tried another tack. 'He's grown up a lot since you last saw him.'

'Who's Matthew?' Tamsin asked rudely.

'You know perfectly well who Matthew is,' Henry snapped, and he closed his mouth in a grim line, determined not to say another word until they reached home.

'There's a girl at school', Tamsin began after a pause, 'whose baby brother bled to death last week.'

'How awful!' said Henry despite himself. 'What happened?'

Tamsin was away: 'Well this baby, which my friend hated because it was always crying, was crawling about on the floor where someone had left a mousetrap – and this mousetrap was set, you see, because, as it so happens, they'd been having the most awful plague of mice. They had them everywhere – in the larder, in the lavatory, under the beds – and they were those absolutely enormous mega-mice, so they thought they ought to poison them but then they couldn't put poison down because of this baby which was always crying and crawling about on the floor, and they thought he might eat this poison if they put it down, so instead they got these traps and they set them all very, very carefully with absolutely delicious bait because they were really determined to catch these whopping mice. So they didn't just put any old cheese rind in the traps, but they put stuff like Camembert and little bits of delicious quiche and Mars Bars and stuff – so this really fat baby, which was the most incredibly greedy baby you have ever seen, which was probably why it was always crying because it was always hungry and it hated all that filthy mush they give babies to eat – and what it really liked was very, very strong French cheeses smelling of wet nappies, and chicken Tikka and

23

those disgusting andouillette things Mum eats in France. Anyway, they put these mousetraps in some places which they thought their revolting fat baby couldn't reach, like behind the television – and – just as its horrid little fat pudgy fingers closed round the most tantalising lump of Roquefort – wham! The great trap was sprung and three little fat fingers were left to tell the tale. They gave the baby the kiss of life and they rushed it to hospital, but it still died. And, do you know, the mother's hair went white just like that – overnight . . .'

'Are you sure this is all true?' Henry asked quietly, when he could at last get a word in edgeways.

'I absolutely promise you. I swear on the Holy Bible. . .'

'If you are going to lie,' Henry said coldly, 'please don't compound the offence with blasphemy.'

'You just never believe anything,' Tamsin said crossly. 'But I promise you it's true – well, I may be wrong about the Roquefort. I don't know exactly what it was they put in the mousetrap.' With that she relapsed into her former sulky silence until they reached the Old Rectory.

Henry sensed that the weekend was beginning just as badly as he had expected. He wondered how Angie would cope. He knew that she dreaded the arrival of Tamsin and sometimes he even suspected that her unease with and dislike or resentment of his daughter bordered on hatred. She never said very much about Tamsin but when she was around, Angie became cold and hard and particularly distant, and she tended to adopt a somewhat sarcastic tone.

As for Henry, his feelings about his daughter were so complicated that it was easier for him not to think about them at all. Waiting for the train at Pewsey, he had been dreading the confusion her visit would obviously bring and then, when he had briefly thought she was not on the train, he had been aware of a momentary sense of relief, followed by one of apprehension. When she **at** last appeared, he felt a surge of pride. Tamsin was very like her mother, but more spectacular, taller and bolder looking. Henry couldn't help recognising that, although he couldn't claim to like the way she dressed, her clothes had style and that she carried herself well. There was something exotic about Tamsin in her crazy mixture of lace and leather and velvet, and something overtly sexual about her bearing from which Henry longed to be able to back away.

When they arrived at the Old Rectory with all its bright, clear colours and clean, cheerful chintzes, they found Angie in the kitchen with Matthew; she was spoon-feeding something pink into her baby's face.

'Hi,' said Tamsin casually, nodding in Angie's direction. She played a game with herself whenever she came to stay with her father, which involved seeing if she could avoid kissing Angie. But Angie was wise to it and, determined not to be put in the wrong herself, she got up from the table where she was sitting and came towards Tamsin with her face outstretched. Tamsin had to kiss her, but she refused to acknowledge Matthew or in any way indicate that she had noticed his presence.

Henry wandered out of the room where the atmosphere was making him feel uncomfortable. He always thought that if he left the two together, they would have to get on. He was also of the opinion that all women liked babies and that therefore Tamsin's hard line about Matthew must eventually melt if she saw enough of him. Henry didn't care for babies himself but he had to admit that as far as they went, Matthew was a nice little fellow.

Brightly and coldly Angie offered Tamsin tea and crumpets, but Tamsin refused both just as coldly, although she would really have loved a crumpet; she hadn't had one for ages. She could not decide whether to go straight to her room or to tell Angie about the fat baby who had been killed by a mousetrap. In the end, she chose the former because, although she would have enjoyed the expression on Angie's face, and although she loved teasing her, she somehow felt that Angie and the baby were not a worthy enough audience for her theatricals. Why should she make the effort just for them? She might wait until there was someone else around too. She wondered which of Angie's friends would make an appearance during the course of the weekend.

Angie was thoroughly relieved when Tamsin left the kitchen and she returned to spoon-feeding Matthew, cooing and talking baby talk with her face pushed right up to his.

Had he any experience of the world, Matthew might have wondered at this great face pushed so close to his and at the soppy drivel pouring like honey from the mouth, while the eyes were cold and hard and the mind was clearly on other matters. As it was, something clearly offended him so that suddenly and incomprehensibly to his mother, he opened his mouth and began to bawl, sending a shower of pink saliva in every direction.

Angie wiped his face and hers as best she could and swept her darling up in her arms so that when Henry came back into the kitchen, hoping to find the ice cracked if not broken, he discovered his wife dancing around the room with a howling baby, cooing, as she did so, 'You mustn't let that horrid girl frighten you . . .'

She broke off as she saw Henry, and the baby, as suddenly as it had started, stopped crying.

'What did Tamsin do?' Henry was beginning to feel cross. There seemed to be trouble already and it wasn't even six o'clock on Friday night. How on earth were they going to get through the weekend at this rate?

Angie smiled prettily at Henry, gave the baby a kiss and said in her usual, sweet, light voice, 'Oh nothing. I'm sure she didn't mean it. He was probably frightened by all those black clothes. And remember, he doesn't know Tamsin. She's virtually a stranger to him.'

'Tamsin can be silly,' Henry conceded. He never really liked discussing Tamsin in any way with Angie. Her inferred criticism of his daughter was too difficult for him to take.

'I've got to make a couple of telephone calls,' he said by way of an excuse, and left the kitchen.

Angie watched him go and, as she did so, her face grew cold and hard again. Henry made her feel very angry at times by his indifference. Tamsin was his daughter – why didn't he do something about her – tell her how to behave? She had no manners at all and only ever thought about herself. Angie couldn't see that there was very much to be gained by her continuously coming to stay. She didn't seem to have a very close relationship with Henry which, in a way, considering Henry's character, wasn't at all surprising, and she certainly had no relationship of any kind beyond a sustained coldness with Angie. The baby she refused to acknowledge. She thought it both rude and foolish of Tamsin to go on minding about her father's annulment. The silly girl never lost an opportunity to make some annoying comment about it. It was nothing to do with her anyway.

Sometimes Angie wished they hadn't bothered about an annulment, but Henry had been insistent. He would never have married her had he not been able to do so with the blessing of the Church. Religion was very important to him, but Angie had never really bothered about it, although she had been strictly brought up as a Catholic and sent to a Catholic convent. Henry used to say to her years ago, when they were first having an affair, that no one could have been brought up like she was and think like she did.

For Angie, the whole paraphernalia of the Catholic Church was something which had never really caught her imagination, or touched her heart. She associated it with unworldly grandmothers and maiden aunts and school and rules and constraint. She, unlike her little sister and so many of her contemporaries at school, had never been caught up in the adolescent emotional desire to become a nun and give herself to God. Angie had always been too worldly, too independent and a flouter of rules. But when she realised that his Catholicism was so important to Henry and that at the same time, marriage to Henry was so important to her, she knew that she would at least have to pay lip service to it, which was precisely what she had done and continued to do. Left to her own devices, she would have married Henry quite happily in a registry office and never set foot in a church again. Even now she felt a little embarrassed when made to think about the annulment. Did Henry really believe that he had never been married to Annie? The idea struck her as rather peculiar.

But marriage to Henry had not turned out quite as Angie had expected, so that within only a few years they had each developed a kind of dull acceptance of each other. Henry had provided all that Angie could possibly ask for materially, including the pretty house which she felt suited her perfectly. Friends came and went and admired it and no doubt admired Angie in it with her red curls, her long neck, delicate jawline and straight nose. She enjoyed social life, loved to flirt madly and be praised. Perhaps all this gave her some sense of her own reality. With her baby, together with whom she sometimes felt she presented the perfect picture of mother and child, she was quite pleased. Despite all this, and without Angie, who was not a reflective person, even realising it, there seemed to be something missing. Perhaps it was just that she had got what she wanted and no longer knew what to aim for.

What she did not want was anything to do with Tamsin ever, for apart from anything else, Tamsin made her feel uneasy, not that she would have admitted that. In any case she didn't feel like making a great effort about the weekend. Tamsin was Henry's responsibility and he could look after her. But when Henry did do something for his daughter, Angie only felt herself growing irritable. He clearly minded about her in a quiet way, and seemed to be almost afraid of her.

People admired Tamsin's looks, but Angie tossed her curls and put her nose in the air and said that she couldn't see what was so special about her. She just looked like all the other girls of her age as far as Angie could see. Henry, on the other hand, was obviously proud of his daughter's appearance, so much so that Angie sometimes felt a little uncomfortable and told Henry that he was making a bit of a fool of himself.

Angie went to put her baby to bed and Henry sat at his desk sorting through some papers, while Tasmin lay in her room with her hands behind her head, staring at the ceiling, listening to her Walkman and hating Angie. Later she went unwillingly down to supper and retold the story of the baby and the mousetrap, but she only told it with half her original verve because in the middle she began to be bored by it herself. Angie looked sarcastic and Henry said nothing, but ate his soup in silence.

On Saturday Tamsin decided that her father deserved to be punished for having anything to do with anyone so frightful as Angie and so she remained in her bedroom with her Walkman for most of the day, although she spent part of the afternoon aimlessly mooching around the vegetable garden.

It was a walled garden, well kept in the summer, but in winter dripping, misty and dank, and smelling of rotting cabbages. There were espaliered apple trees and the paths were bordered with box hedges. A robin pecked at a worm and a few rusty mole traps stuck out of the ground beside a row of purple cabbages growing at awkward, angry angles. This place was so other-worldly that Tamsin loved it. She never came to see her father without visiting the vegetable garden, a peaceful place in which she could allow her imagination to take flight and which she loved like a refuge.

In the evening she said she wasn't hungry and retired to her bedroom again. Angie tossed her head and said that if that was what she wanted, then let her get on with it, but Henry was cross. He went upstairs and banged on Tamsin's door.

Tamsin had locked her door and nothing would make her unlock it. Henry certainly needn't think she would let him in. She didn't want him in her bedroom just now, thank you very much.

Downstairs, Henry said, 'I don't think she can be feeling very well.'

Angie just said, 'Oh, pooh,' and felt relieved that she would not have her stepdaughter's company for supper.

By Sunday morning Tamsin was bored with having spent so many hours in her bedroom so she came down for some breakfast at about half-past nine. Her father was standing in the hall with his overcoat on, ready to go to mass. 'Angie, do hurry up, we'll be late,' he called up the stairs, but when he saw Tamsin, he knew better than to order her into the car. He had had the same battle so often and, whether he won or lost, it seemed to make no difference. Tamsin behaved badly in church by ostentatiously paying no attention to what was going on, by not taking communion and by yawning and stretching during the sermon. At the end of mass, she was always the first out, lighting up an instant cigarette in the church porch. All this made Henry so angry and it was so painful to him that he almost preferred her to stay at home in a pagan hell of her own creating.

Henry blamed Annie for Tamsin's attitude to the Church. He felt that she had never had a properly devout attitude to her faith and he was sure that she had lapsed badly since their separation. He winced slightly when he remembered the subtly mocking look which she used to give him from under her dark lashes whenever he tried to make her think more seriously about her religion. Angie was different – when he had first met her she had been feckless and young – and who could blame her for that? Now she had quite changed and had clearly become more thoughtful so that she took her religion seriously and was as assiduous as Henry in practising it. It absolutely never occurred to him that if he happened to be away on a Sunday, she would stretch languorously and spend the morning in bed with her baby, the *Sunday Times* and a cup of coffee.

Some friends of Henry's and Angie's, a solicitor and his wife, came to lunch and Tamsin was briefly jolted out of her moodiness. Henry felt proud of her as she stood and talked animatedly in front of the fireplace, with a glass of sherry in her hand. She looked splendid and her eyes shone as she talked. Hung around her neck on a leather thong, he noticed a huge black plastic cross. It was not necessarily the one he would have chosen but, not realising that crosses were the fashion among teenagers, he presumed it to be a silent protestation of residual faith, and so was not at all prepared for what came next.

'We didn't see you at mass?' the solicitor's wife enquired innocently.

'Oh, no,' said Tamsin. 'I don't go any more. You see I've lost my faith.'

Mrs Solicitor looked embarrassed and wasn't sure quite what to say, but she need not have worried as Tamsin was only too ready to expand with no further prompting.

'It's all to do with Mum's lover,' she said and everybody looked at the ground except Angie, who left the room on the pretext of attending to the lunch. 'Well she's got this lover,' Tamsin went on, 'who's a journalist so he's always in Ethiopia or Bosnia or somewhere which must be a bit frustrating for poor Mum – but anyway, he was in Iraq at the time of the Gulf War and what he saw was absolutely horrific – you should hear him talking about it – there were these babies still crying with their heads blown off and old men with their eyes hanging out of their sockets on strings – and women whose houses had been bombed, giving birth under enemy fire in the streets of Baghdad . . .'

'I don't think you can have got that quite right,' Henry interrupted, coldly angry.

'Oh yes I have,' Tamsin flared up, her eyes shining even more brightly than before. 'And how can you believe in a God who allows the so-called forces of freedom to go out and ruthlessly massacre and maim unprepared, innocent old men and women and children.'

Luckily, Angie came back at that moment to announce that lunch was ready.

Although in principle Tamsin, who lived with her mother during the week, was supposed to go to her father for three out of four weekends, she in fact, by silent mutual consent, went there far less often and it was with a definite sense of relief that Henry drove her to the station that afternoon. He did not expect she would be back again for a little while.

'Hallo, Fanny? It's Camilla. Have you heard what's happened now?'

'No. What?'

'Well you know that Tamsin went to stay with Henry at the weekend?'

'Mmm . . .'

'Apparently it was an absolute disaster and Angie turned her out of the house so she came home early – and God knows what Henry thinks he's up to . . .'

'How do you know? Who told you?'

'It's most extraordinary, but Henry's wife, Angie, has got a sister – actually she's got dozens of sisters – but one of her sisters happens to be going out with a friend of ours who brought her round here for a drink last night. Sheer coincidence. I've never seen her before in my life – never even heard of her – and then someone said something about Annie, and this girl pricked up her ears and said she'd only been talking to Angie on the telephone half an hour before.'

'So what did she say?'

'Well – apparently Tamsin was absolutely beastly all weekend and she was horrid to the baby and made it cry and she was incredibly rude to Angie. I do really think that Henry ought at least to see that that girl's polite to his wife. I'm really beginning to feel sorry for Angie, you know . . .'

'I agree, it must be terribly difficult for her. Anyway, what happened?'

'Well you know, don't you, that that – awful as it may sound – some of these girls actually enjoy it . . .'

'I can't believe that Camilla.'

'Perhaps you can't, but apparently it's true – and just

33

look at Tamsin. She's very glamorous and, I would say, provocative. So she spends three quarters of the weekend closeted in her room pretending to sulk or something and Henry goes up there and locks himself in with her, claiming to be cajoling her out of her bad mood. I don't like that at all. Do you?'

'Surely he wouldn't do anything with his wife there. Perhaps he really was just trying to talk to her.'

'Fanny, you're so naïve. Anyway, I'm only telling you what Angie told her sister, who told me. I haven't invented it.'

'How awful!'

'The funny thing is that Tamsin's very religious, you know. She's got that in common with her father and I think it brings them very close together. You see, the reason she hated that annulment was because she was so religious – she hated the idea that her parents had been so-called living in sin for all those years. Anyway, I think it must all have started because she and Henry kept having all these tête-à-têtes about religion and they probably got very emotional, and then – you know – one thing leads to another.'

'I suppose you could be right . . .'

III

Sarah was alone at home. She had had an unsatisfactory day and was feeling disgruntled and dissatisfied with her lot. She had had friends to supper the night before and had spent the morning not clearing up the mess in the sitting-room and the kitchen.

The last owners of Sarah's house had discreetly added an extra floor, so that although it was in a parallel and similar street to Annie's, it was a bit bigger and quite unlike Annie's on the inside, because Sarah liked everything to be very neat and pale and modern and stream-lined and aluminium.

After eating a Greek-style yoghurt and half a bar of Chocolat Meunier for her lunch, Sarah had set out to attend her aerobics class, only to find when she got there that it had been cancelled because the teacher had 'flu, and no one had remembered to tell her. She came home crossly and spent the rest of the afternoon belatedly clearing up yesterday evening's mess. Neil was away at a conference in Milan and wouldn't be back until the end of the week and the children had gone back to school so she had the house to herself.

Sometimes Sarah was glad when no one was at home

and she could luxuriate in the freedom to do as she pleased, but lately her pleasure in that freedom seemed to have staled. She didn't have very much to do – or rather, there weren't many things she wanted to do. She loved Neil in a way but not with a passion – nor had she ever – and she certainly did not consider herself to be unhappy with him although she sometimes hankered after her old bachelor days when she had been much courted and admired. She missed the excitement of being taken out to dinner and flirting and wondering whether to say yes or no, and so sometimes played with the idea of taking a lover before it was too late and she lost her looks for ever. Her looks were very important to her and she flattered herself that she did not seem her age. But then, where on earth did you find a lover? She ought to be able to find one in the whole of London, but all the men Sarah knew were either involved elsewhere, gay, or frankly unattractive. One or two were discarded lovers of years gone by.

Sarah had no desire to hurt Neil, but then he was away so often that he really never need know; but one thing that Sarah would not like about having a lover would be the gossip. Her friends were all such dreadful gossips – and they would be bound to get the wrong end of the stick where she was concerned. They never understood her motives nor knew what was going on in her head – let alone her heart. Sometimes even Isabel could be so stupid in the conclusions she jumped to. The thought of Isabel suddenly made Sarah feel rather cross. She wondered if she really was having an affair with Walter. She hoped not, but she had no idea why she hoped not. It wasn't as though she wanted to have anything to do with Walter herself. Of course she didn't. As far as she was concerned Walter was just a very close friend. Nothing more. Anyway, she had always thought that Walter might be gay.

It annoyed Sarah to think of Walter having an affair with Isabel and it annoyed her to think that Walter, who was her friend, whom she'd known years before she even came to live in the Village – her spare man – who confided in her – had not told her about this new development in his life. If it was true, which of course it might not be, she would not be able to avoid the feeling that there was something disturbing about it. It was all very well Isabel thinking that just because she had been widowed early and in tragic circumstances, she had the right to stalk London in search of men.

Sarah began to think of Isabel and Walter together and the thought made her feel tense. She did not want them to be together. She was sitting at her kitchen table disconsolately turning the pages of the *Daily Mail*, not interested in and irritated by everything that met her eye. She looked at her watch. It was seven o'clock and an empty evening stretched ahead of her. She wondered if Walter would be back from work yet and decided to ring him and see.

The telephone rang for some time and Sarah was just about to ring off when Walter answered. Somehow she had not expected him to be in, so the sound of his voice took her by surprise and she didn't know what to say. What had she rung for? She didn't want to ask him round because she didn't want a rebuff, nor did she want to hear that he was going to see Isabel, so she just dropped the telephone back into its cradle without saying a word.

Half an hour later, because she was feeling complicated about what she had done, she decided to try Walter once more. She wanted to dispel the uncomfortable idea that Walter might somehow have guessed that it was she who had rung off so abruptly. This time, after a moment or two, there was a click and Walter's recorded voice said, 'I'm sorry there is no one . . .' Sarah rang off again without saying anything. She looked at her finger-nails. They needed filing so she searched in her bag for an emery board.

As she attended to her nails, her thoughts returned to Isabel. She felt sure that Walter must be round at Isabel's. But how could she be certain? She decided to ring Isabel to find out exactly what was going on. Isabel, unusually, was not in a mood to talk. She was in a hurry, she said, without explaining why.

An hour later Sarah was pouring herself a second gin and tonic. She didn't like drinking alone and didn't usually do it, but today was an exception – she was feeling so tense and disgruntled and everything had gone wrong. She was still thinking about Walter and Isabel. In fact she couldn't get them out of her mind. She felt really offended – she thought justifiably – that Walter hadn't told her what was going on and that she had had to hear about it from Fanny of all people.

It was a bit much, she decided. She would ring Isabel again and interrupt her cosy little supper – or whatever else it was she might be doing. Isabel, it seemed, was really a bit of a snake in the grass. She'd known Walter for long enough without anything coming of it – what on earth had suddenly got into her?

'Are you alone?' Sarah asked as soon as Isabel answered the telephone.

'Yes. Why?' Isabel wanted to know.

'Well, I didn't want to interrupt anything,' Sarah said. 'I wondered if you'd like to come round to supper tomorrow,' she added lamely.

'I'm sorry,' said Isabel. 'I won't be able to – I'm doing something.' She didn't say what, which Sarah thought was definitely suspicious. For that matter, Sarah began to wonder if Isabel had been lying when she said she was alone.

Walter was the kind of man in whom women confide,

which was perhaps what made Sarah suspect him of being gay. Or perhaps it was just because, despite his long and close friendship with her, he had never been especially susceptible to her charms. Sarah was sublimely confident of her ability to attract men and had a tendency to suppose that there must be something odd about them if they didn't fall for her. But had she been honest with herself, she would have realised that throughout their friendship, it had been she who confided in Walter and not the other way round.

Although he had lived alone for most of his adult life, Walter was not lonely. He had had a disastrous early marriage which lasted for only a few years, and when he and his wife finally separated, he felt so immensely relieved to be on his own that he began to wonder if perhaps he was not made for marriage. Who could say what had gone wrong in his, or who was to blame? It seemed to him quite simply that two perfectly decent people had just made an appalling mistake in not realising that they were temperamentally, intellectually and physically quite unsuited to each other. It was a mystery how they had come together in the first place. Perhaps each had reminded the other of someone else, or perhaps they were just around together at a time when marriage seemed to them both like a solution to whatever had gone before.

Walter had always been quite a reserved person who never talked very much about himself, let alone about his failed marriage which now, at any rate, was so far behind him that he hardly ever thought about it any more. He was an archivist whose main subject was geology and for years he had been working quietly away in the Natural History Museum doing nobody knew exactly what. He had lived in the Village for nearly as long as he had worked in the Natural History Museum, was liked by his neighbours, and minded his own business, which was perhaps why he attracted other people's confidences – rather than for the reasons Sarah put about.

Walter was fond of Sarah. He liked her cheerful confidence in her good looks although he suspected it masked some kind of intellectual insecurity. He sort of liked her egoism which allowed him to sit back and relax while she chattered on about this and that and Neil – and the boys and the neighbours, and her need to fulfil herself and about everyone else's inadequacies, and the hideous colour the new neighbours had painted their house and what the man in the newsagent's had said to her on Monday and so forth. He found in her an easy companion and because she was often on her own, he would take her to the cinema or they would have supper together in either his house or hers. It was no secret.

Although he could see that she was very pretty and full of sexual confidence, Walter had never found Sarah attractive. Perhaps he found her insensitivity somewhat daunting, but in any case, he would never have dreamed of having anything to do with another man's wife. He took his pleasures elsewhere, fleetingly and in a sleazier world.

Sarah would have been both puzzled and annoyed if she had known that on the very evening when she kept telephoning Walter and Isabel in turn, Walter was in fact with Annie.

Walter had bumped into Annie as they both emerged from the underground on their way back from work and they had fallen into step.

'I heard from Will on Friday,' she said. 'He's coming back soon. Thank God.'

They chatted about the horrors of the situation in

Bosnia and Walter said that Annie would surely be relieved to have Will back for a while.

Annie laughed. 'If I ever get involved with anyone else,' she said, 'it'll have to be someone with a very safe job which keeps him at home – a grocer or something . . .' They were just reaching Annie's house and she was feeling pleased by Walter's quiet presence. 'Would you like to come in for a drink?' she said. She hadn't seen him for some time and somehow didn't want to let him go.

Walter was tempted. He hadn't anything particular to do that evening but he ought just to go home for a while to make a few telephone calls. He'd love to come back later for a drink. There was a good film on round the corner which he wanted to see, perhaps Annie would like to go with him?

'Funny,' Walter said, when he came back half an hour later, 'I forgot to turn on my ansaphone this morning and just as I got home the telephone was ringing. I answered it in time, but as soon as the person on the other end heard my voice, they rang off. I don't like it when that happens.'

'Not very nice,' said Annie.

Tamsin was hunched in the corner of the sofa reading an article entitled, 'The Last Taboo' in a magazine for teenagers. She didn't bother to look up when Walter came in. She couldn't see why everyone thought he was so wonderful. Seemed pretty boring to her.

Walter said hallo to her and she grunted ungraciously in return, still without looking up. He felt sorry for her, so sulkily hunched there, but rather hoped she wouldn't stay to cast a blight on the atmosphere.

Annie wondered for the umpteenth time how the pretty, happy little girl of only a few years back had turned into this sullen, ill-mannered creature – and then she wondered how many more years of this moodiness she would have to put up with. No one, she had told Tamsin, thought Walter, 'so wonderful'. He was just a nice, friendly neighbour. She said, 'Have you got a lot of homework to do, darling?'

Tamsin took the hint as, in any case, she didn't particularly want to be around Walter and her mother. 'I'm going to Susie's,' she said. 'I'll stay there the night. Her parents are going out.' She left the room and a little while later Annie and Walter heard the front door slam.

'I suppose she really has gone to Susie's,' Annie sighed. 'It's quite impossible to keep checking up all the time. I sometimes think it would be easier if we lived in the country.'

Walter had known Annie only since she came to live in his street; he had met her then through Sarah who, at the time, still lived in Fulham. From the very beginning he found her attractive and particularly liked her frank manner, so that he was always positively pleased when their paths unexpectedly crossed as they had this evening outside the underground. Perhaps it was precisely because of this that he had carefully avoided getting to know her at all well. Besides, Annie was involved with Will who was usually in some far-off, war-torn part of the globe and Walter would not have wanted to interfere in that relationship. He looked at her now and wondered, as he had done occasionally before, what she would be like to make love to. She had a gentle voice. He liked that.

Annie was worried about Tamsin. Lately she could think of nothing else. She found that any form of communication with her daughter had become almost impossible, which difficulty was further complicated by Tamsin's swiftly developing, unbearable habit of telling the most exaggerated tales to everyone about everything. Annie didn't think Tamsin was doing any work at school and she had very little idea of how she filled her hours roaming around the town with her friends. She didn't know if Tamsin took drugs or slept with boys, or stole or drank or what she did. She didn't think she was particularly happy. She certainly didn't look it. And reading between the lines, she suspected the weekend with Henry had been a disaster. She often wished there were someone with whom she could discuss the problem. Now, in addition to everything else, there were these filthy rumours which Sarah seemed to delight in passing on. Annie didn't believe in them for a moment and wanted nothing more than to be able to scotch them, but she did wonder where on earth they could have started, and sometimes even dreaded that they might have sprung from one of Tamsin's own lies.

How could she ask Tamsin about it? It was out of the question, and anyway there was no knowing what credence she could give to anything Tamsin might say in reply. Furthermore, if she herself was not aware of the rumours, Annie certainly didn't want to put any ideas into her head.

Sarah was so busy gossiping and spreading trouble that Annie had no intention whatsoever of talking to her. Once or twice she had nearly rung her mother, but then her mother was so totally out of touch that the whole thing would have required far too much explaining. That left her sister who had many too many problems of her own to have any time for Annie's. So Annie kept her troubles to herself and turned them over and over in her mind, especially during the small hours of the morning. There was Will, of course, but she could hardly share such domestic problems with a man who telephoned every ten days from Sarajevo. She longed for Will and missed him dreadfully, but his prolonged absences in terrible danger zones placed a severe strain on their relationship and made it somehow rather incomplete. So unalike were their day-to-day existences, that it was almost impossible for either of them to imagine themselves in the other's shoes.

It was rather as though Annie lived at a different time in history from any of her friends – at a time when men went to the Crusades, or to build an empire, or even to fight the Germans, leaving the women behind to mind the children and keep the home fires burning. It was unusual nowadays to live as Annie did.

So there was Walter, sitting in Annie's comfortable sitting-room, almost looking as if he belonged there, very much at ease in an unobtrusive way. Annie looked at him and realised that she really did not know him at all well. She knew him through Sarah and she saw him often enough in the street, and he'd been for a drink once with her and Will when Will was at home, and she and Will had met him at Isabel's house once or twice, but she didn't know him. She supposed that she had never been alone with him like this before although she had always found any exchanges with him in the street remarkably easy and not usually confined to banalities about the weather. She liked what he looked like; there was something oddly striking about his appearance. His hair was just brown, with no grey in it as yet, but his eyes which gave his otherwise rather impassive face a somewhat haunted look were very black indeed so that Annie thought perhaps he might have Indian blood. On his left cheek there was a large mole. She wondered for a moment how old he was – late forties – fifty perhaps. And then she found herself wondering, too, what he did for sex, but she decided not to ask Sarah. She suddenly did not want to hear anything that Sarah might have to say on the subject.

Instead, she began quite inexplicably to talk about Tamsin. The words came tumbling out as she found herself telling Walter about her anxieties for her daughter, her fears and her apparent helplessness. She told him about

Henry and Angie and that Tamsin had been to stay with them for the weekend but that she, Annie, had no way of knowing what had happened, whether Tamsin felt happy there or not. She even told him about the horrible rumours which Sarah had been spreading, and she told him that, although there were a lot of things about Henry that weren't very nice, she would never, ever believe that of him — and what was she to do?

Walter just sat and listened, fascinated by watching Annie as she talked. He liked her warmth, passion even, and he liked her forthright unselfconscious manner. He wondered if she had ever realised quite how good-looking she was and he wondered if she was ever really happy. It must be so difficult and lonely being involved with someone who was away so much — and in such frightening places.

'Oh dear,' she suddenly said, jumping to her feet. 'I didn't mean to bore you with all my troubles. I'm so sorry. Let me give you another drink.'

Walter stood up and handed her his glass. He felt like kissing her, but just said, 'What do you feel about going to the cinema?'

They went to the cinema and afterwards wandered up the Bayswater Road to a pizzeria where they had something to eat. They didn't talk about Tamsin any more, but about the film and the street where they lived and what gossips their neighbours were. And then they talked about gossip itself and about whether they thought it could ever change the course of events. Annie laughed a lot which she hadn't done for some time and Walter found himself thinking her rather wonderful.

When Annie said goodbye to Walter on her doorstep, she thanked him warmly for the evening and then, as she shut her front door behind her, she realised that she felt quite different now from how she had felt for a long time.

She was relaxed and almost happy and all her troubles seemed to have shrunk to manageable proportions. She was rather embarrassed to have talked so much about Tamsin to a comparative stranger, but it was a relief to have got it off her chest, and after that she had really enjoyed the evening.

She wondered about Walter. What was it that had made him so easy to talk to? Why did he live alone and what was his history? She thought she remembered Sarah saying he was gay and perhaps he was. It didn't matter to her. But she liked him. He was easy and comfortable. She rather liked the way he dressed, too. He seemed to choose his clothes with care. They looked well made and even fairly expensive but then he wore them with such a disregard for matching colour or style so that more often than not his tie clashed with his shirt, or his socks with his trousers. Annie had noticed this before and been vaguely amused by it. Now she found it rather attractive.

Walter strolled back down the street to his own house deep in thought, hands thrust into his pockets, staring at the ground, he wandered absent-mindedly from side to side of the pavement. Annie, he knew, was not for him, life – fate – luck – whatever – had decreed otherwise.

When Annie woke in the morning she had slept well for once, but on remembering that Tamsin had gone out the night before, she immediately began to worry again about her daughter. She hoped that Tamsin really had gone to stay with Susie and wondered whether to ring Susie's house on some spurious excuse to find out if it was true or not. She hated checking up and knew that, in a way, it was counter-productive and only served to widen the gulf between herself and Tamsin. But what was she to do? She ought to have some control over a fifteen-year-old and she had some right to demand the truth. She picked up the telephone but put it down again without dialling a number. First she would have some breakfast and then she would make up her mind.

Annie worked three days a week, teaching English as a foreign language in a language school in North London. She quite enjoyed the job and did it well, but only the year before, she had given up a far more interesting full-time job which she loved in order to be at home more often for Tamsin. Since Tamsin now absented herself as often as possible from the house, Annie had begun to think that she had shut the stable door too late. She didn't have to go to work today and knew that if she didn't ring Susie's house for reassurance as to Tamsin's whereabouts, she would worry about her all day.

She swallowed the last of her coffee and was just about to pick up the telephone when it rang. She answered urgently, longing for it to be Tamsin, but it was Sarah.

'Are you all right?' Sarah asked with feeling. 'I was worried about you.'

Annie felt annoyed. 'There's no need to be,' she said distantly, wondering what it was that Sarah really had to say.

'Have you seen Isabel lately?' Sarah asked lightly.

'No, I don't think I've seen her since before Christmas,' said Annie.

'And have you seen Walter at all?'

Annie immediately assumed that Sarah must know somehow that she had been to the cinema with Walter the night before, but she was infuriated by Sarah's nosiness and felt not in the least inclined to account to her for her every movement, so she just said, 'I never see him very often. Why?'

'Well, do you know,' Sarah said, 'that Isabel and Walter are having an affair? It's not very nice for me when I'm supposed to be Walter's great friend to be left in the dark and to have to find out from someone like Fanny.'

47

'Perhaps it's not true.' Annie was irritated. 'And anyway, even if it is, why do you mind?'

'Mind? Of course I don't mind.' Sarah had been wrong-footed. 'But how would you feel if you heard things like that about your friends from other people? And anyway, I don't think it's very nice when you think how recently Isabel was widowed. I think she must be quite a superficial person not to have minded more. I'd be simply devastated if Neil hanged himself . . and Walter was round there all last night.'

Annie couldn't help laughing.

'I can't see what's so funny about it,' Sarah went on.

'Look Sarah,' Annie was feeling infuriated now, 'Isabel's been on her own for over a year – she must be lonely and unhappy – why can't she have a friend?'

'Well, for one thing, I've always suspected Walter of being gay,' Sarah said indignantly.

'In that case, I can't see what the problem is.'

Sarah was beginning to think that Annie was in a very odd mood and it must be something to do with being on the edge of a breakdown, so she eventually decided to let the subject drop and moved on to ask about Tamsin and to try to make a plan to meet at the weekend.

'I say, Camilla, it's Fanny.'

'Hi!'

'I must tell you – Sarah's furious you know – about Isabel and Walter.'

'Why should she mind?'

'Oh, I don't know – perhaps because she's always thought Walter was gay – isn't that what she said to you? Anyway she was really annoyed when I told her.'

'Perhaps she's worried about Isabel and how she'll treat him; after all Isabel can be pretty tough and she's already driven her husband to suicide. What do you think she'll do to Walter? And Sarah's quite protective of Walter, you know. I think she sort of regards him as her property.'

'Oh, I'm sure she does. By the way, I saw Walter walking down the Bayswater Road with Annie last night. It was quite late – we'd been out to dinner and were just coming home. What do you think they were up to?'

'Did they see you?'

'I don't think so – we were in the car.'

'How funny! I didn't really think they knew each other very well. I dare say Walter wanted to talk to someone about Isabel – after all, it would be quite worrying being involved with her, don't you think? I mean, after what's happened. And Isabel's not easy.'

'Why do you think he chose Annie?'

'Perhaps because she is rather outside it all. She doesn't see Isabel that much; whereas anything he said to Sarah would be bound to go straight back.'

'I know. I'm beginning to think that Sarah's a bit of a trouble-maker. I'm not sure I really trust her. Do you?'

'I'd certainly tend to be careful what I said to her. She can be tricky.'

'Her real trouble is – as I keep telling you – that she hasn't got enough to do, especially since she sent those children away to school. She couldn't wait to send them.'

'Oh, I know, and all those crocodile tears when they went – and now she spends her whole time on the telephone gossiping . . .'

'I wonder what she says about us . . .'

IV

Tamsin hoped her mother wouldn't check up to see if she really had gone to stay with Susie. It was lucky that boring old Walter, with silly butterflies on his socks, was there to keep her mind on other things. Tamsin knew that her mother wouldn't be at all pleased if she thought she was spending the night with Billy, but she thought her mother was just old-fashioned. After all, Billy's parents didn't mind. In fact if they were away they apparently didn't mind Billy and Tamsin using their bed.

Tamsin admired Billy tremendously, and thought she was very grown-up indeed having a boyfriend of twenty-three. Unfortunately, she mistook his laid-back insolence for sophistication and his casual attitude to personal property and money for intelligence.

Billy was extremely good-looking; he wore his hair in a fey pony-tail and was tall and golden and god-like and fully aware of his beauty. He strutted and swaggered and tossed his head, and stuck out his chin and clenched his cheek muscles and looked at people from beneath lowered eyelids in a vaguely threatening way. He had dropped out of university at an early stage, saying that he had a brilliant idea for making money, and had been living in Chelsea at his parents' house ever since, doing nothing. He played around with drugs and didn't treat Tamsin very well, but because her looks so complemented his, he thought he'd let her stay about for a while until something better turned up.

Sometimes, in her heart of hearts, Tamsin knew that Billy was treating her badly, but at other times she told herself that she was imagining it and that it was just that he was grown-up. An uncomfortable niggling feeling informed her that Annie would not approve of him, although she didn't quite know why; but then Annie knew nothing about Billy who, in any case, had refused to be taken home by Tamsin. Tamsin was certainly in awe of him and without realising it, she was probably afraid of him, too. She was afraid of his bad opinion, afraid of losing him and afraid of him in bed.

For Billy the sexual act was something brutal and greedy, something essential to his vanity and somehow an expression of his own beauty. For Tamsin, it was hurtful, humiliating and frightening, but grown-up. She longed to spend the night with Billy because he was handsome and wonderful, but she longed to lie beside him quietly and for him not to touch her, but this, of course, was something that she dared not whisper to him, or even to her best friend, Susie. She wondered if there was something wrong with her.

Billy's father, who was very rich, having made a fortune out of a chain of junk-food eateries, gave his son a generous allowance which did nothing to encourage Billy to work. But Billy had ideas and was convinced that before long he would have made his own fortune, be master of his own destiny and able to retire to an estancia in South America with a private aeroplane. His best friend was in sex chat lines and Billy was planning to go in with him. You could make a fortune.

Tamsin and Billy were lying in Billy's parents' bed in Chelsea and Tamsin was wondering if she could be bothered to get up and go to school. She felt sleepy and Billy was leaving her alone for the moment and school seemed so uninviting and so boring.

Billy was lying on his back with his hands behind his head, staring at the ceiling, wondering if he could persuade Tamsin to come and work for the chat line. Billy's friend was having a certain amount of difficulty getting enough girls for the job. You could find them quite easily but the trouble was how to keep them. Too many of them would only stick at it for a couple of days before they started whingeing about being used and not liking what they had to listen to and then they left. What the hell did they expect when they took on the job? Billy couldn't see what their problem was. He thought he might have a certain amount of difficulty convincing Tamsin, but he was sure that he would be able to put on the pressure and in the end get his way. If Billy could involve Tamsin, he felt he would have gained some credibility with his friend who would then be keener to take him on as a partner.

'I say, Tams, I've just had an idea,' he began in an artificially optimistic voice.

Tamsin stirred sleepily and grunted.

'It's a brilliant idea and you could make loads of money.'

Tamsin opened her eyes. She never had enough money.

'You'd be brilliant at it, too,' Billy went on. 'It's a cinch – you know anyone could do it, really – you just have to be yourself.'

Tamsin was beginning to wonder what on earth he was talking about.

Billy had never mentioned the chat line to Tamsin

before, partly because he felt instinctively that she wouldn't like it and that she didn't like his friend, Dirk, either. He had told her that he and Dirk were involved in some business together, but had only referred to it darkly with an air of secret importance. Tamsin, who wasn't remotely interested in business, had never bothered to enquire further.

Billy began to explain the chat line in a roundabout way. There were all these lonely people out there with no one to talk to, with really big problems and no one to tell them to. All they needed was to hear a nice, kind, sympathetic voice down the end of the line. Someone they could share their troubles with, talk to about things that they couldn't mention to anyone else, like sex and stuff. Of course these chat lines were serving a really useful purpose. If these guys didn't have some way of venting their frustration, they'd probably go out and rape someone – or kill them – or both.

Tamsin was inclined to believe the bit about rape and murder and she felt quite a thrill at the idea of playing a part in its prevention. She also felt a prurient thrill at the idea of what exactly might be said on the line. She could do with the money and she liked the idea of doing something of which both her parents would surely disapprove – even if she never bothered to tell them about it. To work on one of these so-called chat lines would give her a feeling of independence, of having taken her life in her own hands and to a certain extent of having flouted society, all of which appealed to her. Nevertheless, there remained at the back of her mind a niggling fear that there might be more to it than she expected. But what the hell? She could get out of it again if she felt like it.

Billy was pleasantly surprised by how easy it was to co-opt Tamsin. He hoped she would stick to the job for a while, but he was fairly confident that he would be able to see to it that she did – at least for long enough to suit his purposes. The only trouble was that he must get it fixed quickly before she changed her mind. He didn't want her going home to her mother and blabbing about it. Her bloody mother would be bound to try to put a stop to it.

He decided that the best thing would be to persuade Tamsin to skip school and go round that very morning to see Dirk.

'You'll get to like Dirk,' he said deceitfully. 'I know you think he's rather unfriendly and arrogant . . .'

Tamsin didn't think anything of the sort. She thought he was creepy, oily and licentious.

'. . . but he's not at all when you get to know him. He's a really sensitive person – it's just that he's rather shy. I think I'd better give him a ring and we can go round and see him straight away.' Billy reached out for the telephone beside his parents' bed. The handset was shaped like a well-known cartoon dog.

Tamsin felt excited, and glad that the decision about whether or not to go to school had been taken out of her hands. Half an hour later, as she climbed into Billy's low-slung, red two-seater, she felt very grown-up. Behind them in the Chelsea house she and Billy had left a far from grown-up mess of an unmade bed, dirty dishes, a lighted gas ring, overflowing ashtrays, open drawers, spilt milk and an unflushed lavatory. Billy had left some dope on the kitchen table and forgotten to lock the basement door into the area.

In the end Annie funked it. She supposed she was a coward and even wondered whether she took her responsibilities as a parent seriously enough, but she simply couldn't face hearing that Tamsin had been lying about staying with Susie. Neither could she face the thought of Tamsin's furious disdain if she discovered that her mother had been checking up on her, particularly if she had been telling the truth all along. That would only be another hole breached in Annie's weakening defences. Really she ought to try talking to Tamsin and asking her about her life, but she had learned from experience that her daughter would only leap into some flight of fantasy as soon as the going became difficult.

Annie was glad that she had talked to Walter about Tamsin and only hoped that she hadn't bored him, but in her heart of hearts she knew that she really ought to speak to Henry. The prospect of having to talk to Henry about anything filled her with gloom so that whenever the need arose – which it inevitably did from time to time over Tamsin – she tended to procrastinate. What sort of relationship, she wondered, did Henry and Tamsin really have? She imagined it to be a distant, fairly surperficial one, since Henry was not only hidebound by his religious principles, but had never been much of what is nowadays called a communicator.

But Annie knew she might be wrong. Life had a way of endlessly taking one by surprise and, try as one might, one could never be sure of how even one's nearest and dearest were thinking. Tamsin and Annie never discussed Henry; in fact the closest they ever came to the subject was when Tamsin made some disparaging remark about Angie. Annie never reacted, she felt it was beneath her to make any comment about Henry's wife.

Annie had been very unhappy at the time of her separation and divorce, suffering from all the usual feelings of rejection, of having been chucked out like an old pair of shoes. She had felt unloved and unworthy of love and, at the time, she had also felt very angry with Angie who, it seemed, had set out single-mindedly and systematically to prise Henry away from her. As for the annulment, she regarded that as total phooey. Whenever she thought about it, it still made her seethe with rage. How could Henry really suppose that the God in whom he claimed to believe so ardently could forgive him his adultery whilst condoning the lies put about in his defence by Henry himself and some sanctimonious Father O'Liebag who hoped to gain a kind of specious popularity from the affair. On whose authority did God prefer the dissembler to the adulterer? And how could intelligent people believe, as they undoubtedly persuaded themselves to do, that lies could actually alter the truth?

Beyond any question of doubt, Annie had been properly married to Henry in the eyes of the Church. Annie knew that even if Henry didn't acknowledge it now, he had once known it to be true. She remembered with distaste Henry in bed, lying on top of her and talking about the sanctity of marriage and what a difference it made and she began to feel slightly queasy. She envied Angie nothing.

Even before the divorce, perhaps from the very earliest days of her marriage, Annie had realised that theirs was an uneasy relationship – probably one that should never have been blessed by the Church or ratified in any way; but it had been. It was true that she had married Henry on the rebound, but on the rebound from someone with whom, she later came to realise, she would have probably been far more unhappy than she had been with Henry.

In fact Annie could not say that she had really been unhappy with Henry until Henry had fallen in love with Angie. Up till then she had been perhaps a little uncomfortable at times, and at times sad, but although she married him *faute de mieux*, she thought long and hard before doing so. Henry was an old friend whom she had never found particularly exciting but whom she believed to be steady, reliable and honourable. But in these three things she had been deceived; perhaps his kind of smooth good looks should have made her more wary.

Henry, on the other hand, had at the time long been harbouring what he assumed to be a useless passion for Annie. Her cool, detached manner had always made him hesitate to approach her, but when her engagement was suddenly broken off, he found the courage, in a rare moment of spontaneity, to make a move. When accepted, he was overjoyed, but being a man who lacked self-confidence, amazed too. For all his good looks, and superficial good manners, Henry had never been able to break free from the inner constraints of fear and uncertainty which had always been, for one reason or another, intrinsic elements of his make-up, and which probably contributed to his blind acceptance of a religion without which he would have felt quite uprooted. Merely to be in a room with other Catholics made Henry feel at home. He sought them out and surrounded himself by them; their very presence gave him a validity of his own. Catholicism for him was a club to which only the chosen belonged and it never crossed his mind for one moment that some of his cousins or old school friends might not believe in God. None of them perhaps. Not one of them.

What Henry lacked was anything approaching a free spirit; everything he thought and did was circumscribed not so much by a belief in God and the tenets of Christianity, as by his belief in the Catholic Church. Annie, for her part, had a far more Protestant attitude to her religion. Although she, too, had been brought up as a Catholic, she had never been able to accept totally what she saw as a package deal. Neither had she ever found it very easy to deceive herself or to deny what had really happened. These days, she rarely went to mass, but would still have written 'RC' on any form enquiring into her religion.

It had always seemed to Annie that it was precisely this absence of a free spirit which stood in the way of any real possibility of communication between herself and Henry. For him everything, every decision he ever took, every idea he ever had – almost down to what he ate for breakfast – was overshadowed by a blindly adhered to ideology at which he had never ever dared to look too closely.

But such was Annie's attitude to marriage that, for all its faults, she would have kept hers going through thick or thin for as long as she possibly could, and if Henry had not fallen so helplessly in love with Angie, and if Angie had not been so ruthlessly determined to get him, she, Annie, would surely have still been with him. For all that, after the break-up and as soon as she began to recover from the pain and the shock, she started to realise that what she was feeling was an immense sense of relief. She was perfectly aware that the path that lay ahead was full of pitfalls and uncertainties, but for nothing in the world would she take Henry back in the unlikely event of his wanting to come.

If it were not for Tamsin, Annie supposed that she would no longer ever see or talk to Henry. She also supposed that he, too, would rather not have anything to do with her. He knew exactly what she thought about his having insisted on an annulment and she had not failed to notice that when she did see him, he had some difficulty in looking her in the eye.

Reluctantly Annie decided that she would ring Henry that evening. She had funked checking up on Tamsin's whereabouts last night, but perhaps, in any case, it would be more profitable to speak to Henry, to ask him how the weekend had gone and generally to share her anxieties with the one other person whose concern they were.

Angie answered the telephone and told Annie that Henry was out. He had gone to see Father Leatham to discuss the problem of a local Anglican clergyman who was being driven over to Rome by his own church's acceptance of women priests. No one should have been happier than Henry at the prospect of a miracle which would once and for all bring the entire errant church back to the true religion. But in this case Henry was profoundly distressed because the clergyman in question was hoping to become a Catholic priest and there was talk of him and others of his kind being allowed to keep their wives and to dispense the sacrament, which, to Henry's way of thinking, would be quite opposed to the teachings of the Church. Annie wondered if she didn't detect a note of sarcasm, even a faint sneer, in Angie's voice as she recounted all this.

Annie didn't give a damn about women priests and neither could she see what on earth the whole matter had to do with Henry, but she knew him well enough and she could see that it was all right up his street, so that he would no doubt spend many a long hour closeted with Father Leatham, reiterating his prejudices and being congratulated on them by the priest.

When Annie did eventually speak to Henry, he was surprisingly friendly and apparently glad to hear from her. He, too, had been worried by Tamsin, particularly at the weekend, and would be glad to discuss the matter with Annie, not that there was probably much they could do, but at least some kind of consistency in their dealings with her would probably be a good thing.

Henry and Annie agreed to meet for lunch at the end of the week.

When Henry turned up at the restaurant, Annie was already seated at a small round table by the window, reading the menu. She looked up as he approached the table and was shocked by the changes she perceived in him. He seemed much thinner than when she had last seen him, drawn and colourless. She wondered if he was happy. If Angie had come out in her true colours, she doubted that he could be.

'How's Matthew?' she asked.

Henry was pleased that Annie asked after his son, which was more than Tamsin would ever do, but he merely replied coldly that the baby was doing very well, thank you. He never felt comfortable with Annie now and he felt particularly uneasy at any mention of his new family. Annie, it seemed, managed in some indefinable way to make him almost dislike her so that he preferred not to look her in the eye; but it never crossed his mind that this hesitancy on his part might have something to do with the way he had treated her. He thought that it was probably her renegade attitude to her religion which caused the trouble and which made her quite unapproachable, and that was what he had come here to discuss today.

It seemed to Henry that none of Tamsin's problems would have come about had she been sent to a proper Catholic school. He blamed himself for not having insisted on it earlier and for having allowed her to go instead to a state comprehensive. He couldn't think why he had agreed so readily.

'Well,' said Annie, 'it was much cheaper for one thing.' Henry was rich, but he never liked spending money.

He looked up from the large menu and over his half-moon reading glasses at Annie. 'It had nothing to do with money,' he lied.

Annie wanted to laugh but instead she merely pointed at his spectacles and said with a smile, 'When did you get those?'

'I can't see a thing without the damn things these days,' he said irritably as he removed them from his nose and held them at arm's length for a moment before replacing them.

Henry was proud of his looks and Annie thought it must annoy him to have to wear glasses. But when the wine came, he clearly began to feel a little more comfortable – he had a prop it seemed. In any case, he sipped it, stared deeply into the bowl of the glass, and asked Annie what she thought of it. She agreed that it was delicious.

By the time the food came, Henry was prepared to tell Annie what he had come to tell her. He even needed his spectacles to eat, she noticed, as he peered hard at a forkful of sole.

Tamsin had appalled Henry when at the weekend she had quite flippantly announced in front of some friends of his – good Catholics – that she had lost her faith. For a while now he had had a certain amount of difficulty in persuading her to accompany him and Angie to mass on Sundays, and when she did go, she appeared to have not the slightest idea how to behave. All this he found deeply disturbing. On top of all that she was a terrible liar, having little, if any, regard for the truth. Then, to add insult to injury, she referred to her mother having a lover in the glibbest of possible fashions. Now Henry knew Annie's private life was no concern of his . . .

Indeed it was not. Annie's eyes flashed.

. . . It had, however, always been agreed that Tamsin should have a proper Catholic upbringing and this was where Henry felt that Annie was to blame.

'Perhaps it would have helped if we had called her Bernadette in the first place, instead of some silly secular name like Tamsin,' Annie remarked archly.

'If you remember, I tried to stand out for a saint's name at the time – Teresa or Claire might have been nice.'

Annie would have liked to take her plate of fish and press it slowly into his face. She restrained herself, however, and merely said, 'Yuk!'

But Henry had started, so he would go on. Annie, he felt, was not living up to her part of the bargain: by failing to take Tamsin to mass and by living openly with a man to whom she was not married she was setting their daughter a bad example, and who could blame the child if her own behaviour was consequently unconventional?

Annie could not remember when she had last felt so angry. She dared not speak lest she explode, so she looked at her plate and ate her fish in icy silence.

Henry continued. What he had in mind was that for the sixth form, Tamsin should be sent to board in a convent. She would be sixteen in May and would be taking her GCSEs in June; that would give them plenty of time to find somewhere for her before September. From now onwards, Annie was to undertake to make sure that Tamsin went to mass on Sundays. If she would not agree, the matter would have to be decided by the solicitors.

It occurred to Annie that Henry was right out of his mind. How could he possibly imagine that you could start ordering someone to church at the age of sixteen? He'd admitted that he was already having difficulty about it himself. She knew perfectly well, too, that Tamsin would quite simply refuse to set her foot inside a boarding-school, let alone a convent, and neither did she blame her. In fact, it was doubtful whether Tamsin would even agree to stay on at school for the sixth form. She might well not qualify anyway, judging by the amount of work she was doing at the moment.

'I think you're being extraordinarily unrealistic,' she said, and wondered why on earth she had bothered to meet Henry at all, if it was only to listen to such nonsense. There seemed to be no way into his brain, no way of dodging past the mountain of hypocrisy and preconceived ideas, so as to impregnate his intelligence and ignite one spark of genuine understanding about his daughter. 'If that's the way you feel,' she went on, 'I suggest you talk to Tamsin yourself. I think it would come better from you.'

By the time the coffee came, neither of them could think of anything more to say and each of them was longing to get away. They both regarded the other as completely unreasonable. As they left the restaurant, a woman at another table waved cheerfully at Annie. Annie vaguely recognised the face, but she had no idea who the woman was. She waved back distractedly.

'Fanny! I haven't heard from you for days. What you been up to?'

'Oh, nothing much. All the usual things – Sainsbury's – and then yesterday I had to go and see my father. He's not very well, really. He hasn't been the same since he had his operation.'

'I've been trying to ring you, but you've been out all the time. Do you know that a friend of mine was having lunch in a restaurant in Chelsea – and guess who was there too?'

'Having lunch with this friend of yours?'

'No, no, no. At another table.'

'I can't guess. A man or a woman.'

'Well both, actually. But the woman's the one we all know.'

'Sarah?'

'No, not Sarah – and by the way, I've got something to tell you about her in a minute.'

'So who was it then?'

'Annie – and she was with this outstandingly good-looking man. This friend of mine doesn't really know Annie very well. She met her in our house once. It must be over a year ago now, but anyway, she saw Annie in this restaurant and the funny thing was that Annie looked really sheepish and clearly didn't want to be seen.'

'So who was the man?'

'I've no idea, but I'll find out. Apparently he was incredibly good-looking.'

'Lucky Annie.'

'You can't blame her, can you, when Will's always away? She needs something to cheer her up.'

'So, Camilla, what were you going to say about Sarah?'

'Oh, Sarah – she's in a dreadful state. She's been having these appalling headaches for the last few days, so she's gone off to have a brain scan. It's very worrying. It appears that she may lose the sight of one eye.'

'How awful . . . poor Sarah. And do you know what I've heard?'

'What?'

'This friend of ours we saw last night – he knows Henry and Angie quite well and he seems to think they're in a pretty bad way . . .'

'That's hardly surprising, if what we hear is true . . .'

'No, nothing to do with the abuse and all that . . .'

'Fanny, do be careful what you say.'

'I'm sure nobody's tapping my telephone.'

'I'm sure they're not, but there might be a crossed line.'

'They wouldn't know who Henry and Angie are – anyway, what this man was saying was that Henry's lost so much money in Lloyd's that he's going to have to sell up and leave that lovely house, which won't please Angie at all – and she may even leave him.'

'Angie leave Henry – really? Or perhaps she's leaving him because of the other thing – you know . . .'

V

'Hallo Sarah, it's Fanny.'

'Hi! How're you?'

'Fine. 'nd you?'

'Oh, I'm all right – except I've been having these beastly headaches.'

'Poor you. What do you think is the matter?'

'Oh, nothing much really. I expect they'll be better in a day or two. I went to see the doctor yesterday and she said it was just sinus. It was so painful the other day that I really thought I must have a brain tumour or something. I was quite ready to have to go for a brain scan. It's not so bad today. Anyway, what's the news?'

'Well, who's this incredibly good-looking man Annie's been seen around with?'

'Annie? I've no idea.'

'I thought you'd be bound to know. Apparently they were seen wining and dining last week, quite engrossed in one another. And Annie was really embarrassed. She didn't want to be seen at all – she cut this other friend of hers dead.'

'That sounds very unlike Annie.'

'I know, but perhaps he's a married man.'

'Who told you about it anyway?'

'Oh, I can't say.'

'Why not?'

'I don't think you know the person, so there's no point.'

'I'm certainly going to ask Annie about it. I'm sure she'll tell me.'

'She may well not, you know. If it is a married man, she wouldn't want it gossiped about.'

'Oh, come on Fanny, you know I wouldn't dream of gossiping about my friends. It's just that she might want to talk to somebody about it, and after all, I am one of her oldest friends. I'm sure she's worried about her relationship with Will in any case. After all, where is it going? He's never around. And I've never ever thought they were remotely suited to one another. I wouldn't want to be unkind, but I don't really think Annie's got the measure of Will. He's a very interesting man, Will. He used to be quite a friend of mine and I really don't see that set-up lasting. Annie's too low-key for Will. You know, he needs somebody more vital – more energetic. I adore Annie – you know I do – but I can't help thinking that he'll get bored with her. For all we know he's already found some doe-eyed Italian aid worker. That's probably why he never comes back. But I'm certainly going to find out who this man is that Annie's seeing.'

'I'd be quite interested to know, if you do find out. I wonder what poor Tamsin makes of it all.'

'I don't know. In any case I think it's time somebody did something about Tamsin. That child needs taking in hand. In fact I think she ought to be having counselling.'

'Of course she should. I can't think why Annie hasn't done anything about it. I mean, if it's true about the abuse – if it's true – that kind of thing wrecks a person's life you know.'

'It's bound to, isn't it? But then, look at Tamsin, she's a very attractive girl. I wouldn't put it past her – I mean would you? – to have egged Henry on? I should think she's quite a little siren.'

'Do you think she's jealous of her mother? Perhaps she egged Henry on in order somehow to score a point over Annie.'

'I wouldn't be surprised at anything.'

When Tamsin saw Dirk that morning, she stared hard at him and didn't like what she saw any more than she had done before. She hated the way he looked at her, his little pig eyes lingering over her body, and she loathed the way he looked at the floor or out of the window, dragging on a cigarette, whenever he talked to you. She was rather frightened of him because she felt him to be cold. As cold as ice.

'These blokes,' he said, 'you've gotta feel sorry for them, yeah. They've got problems and all you have to do is to go with them.' He dragged on his cigarette again, his eyes fixed this time on the toe of a shiny slip-on shoe. He had his right foot nonchalantly balanced on his left knee. With his left hand he fiddled almost nervously with the tassel on the shoe.

Tamsin was beginning slightly to dread this new job she had agreed to do, but she badly wanted the money. She drew comfort from the fact that she had only agreed to do it twice a week to begin with. It meant skiving off school which might be difficult as she had already forged so many notes from her mother that questions were soon bound to be asked. The other problem was that the line would be switched through to her home and she was to work from there which meant, of course, guaranteeing that Annie was out, but it also meant that she might be caught at home when she shouldn't be there by someone ringing her mother. Annie worked two mornings and one afternoon a week and they were usually the same days each week, but she did, very occasionally, alter her timetable which made it all rather risky. And what if Annie were off sick? She wasn't often sick, but you couldn't be certain.

'No problem there. Just make sure that you get to the phone first,' said Dirk, his eyes still fixed on the toe of his shoe.

They were in the sitting-room of Dirk's penthouse flat somewhere near Maida Vale. Tamsin looked around her. It was a funny sort of place, she thought, in a funny sort of area. There was very little furniture in the room which was quite large. Dirk sat in a swivel chair behind a big, untidy desk on which were computers and faxes and telephones and overflowing ashtrays. Billy and Tamsin sat in cheap-looking, dirty, modern armchairs. The carpet was white and grubby and on it, in one corner of the room, stood a huge, dusty, dying yucca in a plastic container. There was only one picture in the room; it was a poster of a stylised fire engine, in an aluminium frame, hanging crookedly from the middle of the wall opposite two small windows.

Tamsin imagined herself in her mother's green-striped sitting-room, surrounded by all her mother's pretty, middle-class things, diving for the telephone, knocking her mother over in her attempt to get to it first. Then she imagined Annie's quiet, cultivated tones in the background, asking 'Who is it, darling?' as some strange, undefined, faceless creature spoke intimately of sex and led her with him down the twisted paths of his imagination. She had cold feet.

'You're not frightened are you?' Dirk sneered. He flicked a hand across his hair, which, stiff with gel, stuck up from his head in a solid block, then reached for another cigarette from the packet on the desk in front of him. 'And you're not going to start being shocked I hope.'

'Of course not,' said Tamsin. She didn't like Dirk's manner, nor did she like the inference that she was only a schoolgirl and not properly grown-up. 'Why should I be shocked? My aunt, you know, is a call-girl. She's got this absolutely incredible flat in Piccadilly or somewhere and it's entirely decorated in pink – pink – pink everywhere – and there are mirrors on all the ceilings, even on the dining-room and kitchen ceilings . . .' Tamsin was off in the land of her own fantasy.

'Okay,' said Dirk languidly. 'You'll do, but we're not interested in your auntie, yeah. You can keep her for story time.'

Tamsin felt a surge of rage welling up in her. How dared this creep patronise her – after all, he needed her services and she considered that she was doing him a favour agreeing to work for his beastly chat line. She stood up and tossed her thick hair back with a haughty gesture.

'C'mon Billy,' she said, 'let's go.'

Billy wanted to stay and discuss business with Dirk, besides he was annoyed and embarrassed by Tamsin's naïveté. He needed to re-establish his street cred with his friend but on the other hand, he felt he had to follow her out now, just in order to reinforce her decision to do the job and to remind her that she must be at home waiting for the phone to ring on Monday morning.

'What d'you want to go and tell Dirk all that crap about your aunt for?' Billy asked angrily, as they went down in the lift.

Tamsin said nothing but instead took a leaf out of Dirk's book and stared superciliously at the floor. When they reached the ground floor, she left the lift and the building with a flounce and hurried off down the street.

She had decided to go to school after all. She had had enough of Billy and Dirk and chat lines for the moment.

Billy hurried along behind her. Suddenly the tables seemed to have been turned, so that he was the weak one, pleading with Tamsin, asking her where she was going, begging her not to be silly but to get into his car, reminding her above all not to forget that she was starting work on Monday. They reached a crossroads and Tamsin jumped onto a bus just as the lights turned to green, to be carried away in the wrong direction, quite unaware of where she was going. She turned to look back just in time to see Billy slouching off disconsolately, hands in pockets, shoulders hunched, back towards where he had left his car. Suddenly he didn't seem so threatening and as the bus hurtled on she felt a wave of optimism. She could cope with Billy and Dirk and the chat line and her mother and father, too – and she would soon have some money in her pocket to boot.

When Tamsin eventually arrived at school, the first person she bumped into in the main corridor was her form teacher.

'So where were you at registration this morning?' the teacher asked icily.

'Well, this awful thing happened,' Tamsin began her story without hesitation. 'Mum had just left for work and I was in the kitchen and I just happened to be juggling with these onions, and I threw one of them too far and it broke the kitchen window. I couldn't leave it, or Mum would have been furious, so I had to spend hours trying to find someone to mend it . . . anyway, in the end, I got this man . . .'

Suddenly Tamsin became aware of the teacher's frosty silence which was apparently quite impervious to the mounting drama of her tale. She broke off her story. 'I'll bring a note from Mum in the morning,' she said.

'Don't bother with that,' said the teacher. 'Just bring the builder's receipt.'

As Walter stepped out of the underground at Notting Hill Gate, he looked around hopefully for Annie. It was on this day last week that he had bumped into her and in the intervening days he noticed that his thoughts kept returning to her with remarkable regularity. He didn't see her getting off the train, and neither was she there on the escalator. He felt childishly disappointed. After all, if he wanted to see Annie he had only to telephone her, but in his heart he felt that this was something he ought not to do. Their meeting last week had been so casual, almost accidental – and of course quite innocent, but if he were to ring her now, it would not be quite so innocent. And he knew it. Walter found himself wondering about the nature of Annie's relationship with Will. He wondered whether, in both their minds, it was a permanent arrangement, or a makeshift, undecided, undefined affair. For a fleeting moment he allowed himself to think of Will, shot dead out there in Sarajevo, caught in the cross-fire between Serb and Muslim. He saw the headlines in the papers, 'British journalist murdered'. But it was just a fleeting thought. Quite fleeting.

When he got home he turned on the answer machine. There was only one call – from Sarah. She spoke in a cross, unfriendly voice. 'I've been trying to get hold of you. Please ring me,' she said. He wondered what on earth the matter was with Sarah. She had been acting most peculiarly lately. He didn't feel like ringing her back if she was going to be in that kind of aggressive mood, but, at the same time, he hated to think that there might be some kind of unexplained misunderstanding between him and a friend. He thought he'd have a bath before deciding what to do next.

In the bath, Walter found himself thinking about Annie again. If Sarah was going to be so unpleasant, he wouldn't be seeing much of her for a while. Perhaps it wouldn't hurt to ring Annie just this once. After all, there could be nothing wrong with taking her to the cinema when they were both alone. Of course the gossips would make something of it if they were seen. Walter knew that for some reason Annie was already tremendously gossiped about and, for all he knew, he, as a single, perhaps rather mysterious man, was gossiped about too.

After his bath Walter took some time to decide what to wear. It couldn't have mattered what he put on because he wasn't going anywhere, but for some reason he was unable to make up his mind about a shirt. Eventually he chose a dark blue one he'd been given for Christmas and hadn't worn yet. It looked fresh and inviting. When he was dressed he decided to ring Sarah and get it over with. He wouldn't ring Annie. It wasn't really a good idea.

Something about Sarah's forbidding manner prevented Walter from asking what the matter was with her. Or perhaps he was just not prepared to play her games.

'I don't ever see you any more,' Sarah wailed.

As far as Walter was concerned, he saw Sarah just as often as he ever did. He'd even had supper with her and Neil at the weekend.

'I suppose it's boring here, and', she insinuated, 'there are other places you would rather be.'

Walter was fed up. He rang off as soon as he decently could and almost before he realised what he was doing, he had looked up Annie's number and was dialling it.

Annie was busy marking some papers when the telephone rang. She didn't mind her job, quite liked and was amused by her students who came from all over the world – more and more from Eastern Europe nowadays, and even Russia – but she missed her old job. Last year she had been working as a picture researcher for a firm specialising in the publication of educational books and encylopaedias. She had loved the work and liked the people she worked with, but she had eventually told herself that she spent too much of her time away from home and didn't devote nearly enough of it to her daughter. So she had sadly resigned, fallen back on an old qualification, and taken this job teaching English.

Tamsin was upstairs at the moment, skulking in her room, and Annie supposed that at any minute she would come out to make a dive for the telephone. The telephone always seemed to be for Tamsin these days. In fact one of the reasons why Tamsin had disappeared to her room in such a particularly bad temper just now was because of a quarrel with her mother over the installation of a second line in the house. Suddenly Tamsin wanted her own private telephone line in her bedroom. Annie certainly wasn't going to pay for that, however hard she was pressed. Tamsin thought her mother was being most unreasonable and retired to her room to mull over new ways of putting pressure on Annie to change her mind.

The telephone rang and rang, and, for what seemed like the umpteenth time that evening, Annie underlined in red the sentence, 'I am staying in England during six months.' She sighed and put down her pen but just as she got to the telephone, it was answered by Tamsin.

Tamsin came downstairs and said with an ungracious grunt, 'It's for you. You might have answered it.' Then she added darkly and rudely, 'I'm off duty,' and she stomped off angrily upstairs back to her bedroom where she lay down on her bed and burst into tears.

Annie's heart lifted up when she heard Walter's sane and friendly voice; it seemed such a welcome interruption of the unbearably tense and claustrophobic atmosphere in the house, where her relationship with this daughter for whose sake she was spending so much more time at home was becoming increasingly difficult. There seemed to be no chink in the armour of Tamsin's self-defence through which her mother could hope to approach her. Annie was beginning to think it would be better if she spent less, rather than more time with her daughter. But, at the same time, she was sure that Tamsin needed her help, if only this apparently insurmountable barrier of non-communication could be broken.

Walter asked Annie how she was, told her that he'd been very busy at work but that he'd enjoyed their evening together and had been thinking about the film they'd seen. He wondered if she would like to go to another one one of these days. There was a good film coming to the cinema on the corner next week. He asked after Tasmin without making any reference to anything that had been said about her when they last met. He didn't quite dare to ask Annie out to supper.

Annie found herself talking easily to Walter and even wondering if she might invite him round to have supper with her, but she thought better of it. She had to get on with her marking and, anyway, there was no accounting for how Tamsin might behave in her present mood.

But they made an arrangement to meet at the weekend.

Annie marked a few more papers and then decided that the atmosphere in the house was so oppressive that she must get out, if only to walk around the block. The time of year didn't help and, although people were beginning to say that the evenings were getting lighter, it seemed to her that they only spoke out of some kind of mad, blind optimism. It was still more than two months before the clocks were due to be put forward and it was foggy. Annie loathed these winter months. She thought as she walked briskly round the block, hunched up against the cold, of Will in Sarajevo where, the papers said, there were inches of snow and sub-zero temperatures. She wondered about the future of her relationship with him. She thought she loved him and she often badly missed him, but she sometimes felt strangely indifferent to him. When she felt like that she was afraid because it seemed then as if she only existed in some kind of icy vacuum where she reacted to her everyday existence automatically and without feeling, like some lifeless robot.

Sometimes Annie thought that although Will was certainly fond of her, loved her in his way, she played such a secondary role in his life that their relationship must be doomed. His job and adventure were everything to him so that when he was away, she probably hardly existed for him. Despite the difficulties of the situation, she could not help thinking that, if he really wanted to, he could manage to contact her more often than he did, even from war-torn Sarajevo. Out of sight, out of mind. He did not begin to comprehend her solitude or the nature of her anxieties about Tamsin and she did not think it right to burden him with such trivia. When Will came home, he was always welcomed like the returning hero she felt him to be and he would arrive, joyous and half drunk with life, to find her waiting there to put her arms around him. *Repos du guerrier*. Would this turn out to be enough in the end, she sometimes asked herself.

Just as Annie turned back into her street, somewhat refreshed by the cold night air and the briskness of her walk, she saw Walter coming out of his front door. He hurried down the steps and turned to walk in her direction.

'Annie!' Walter realised that he sounded ridiculously pleased at meeting his neighbour who, after all, had been no more than a mere acquaintance before last week. He thought Annie must think him a fool.

'I was just off to Oddbins to buy a bottle of wine,' he said by way of explanation. 'Cold, isn't it?'

Annie agreed, but said that she'd had to get out of the house. She'd needed a breath of air.

Walter wanted to ask her in for a drink, but felt silly, standing there shivering on his way to Oddbins.

Annie didn't want to go back indoors to face Tamsin's moodiness and she half sensed Walter's unease. She wished they could go off together for the evening. They were obviously both alone – and lonely, perhaps.

'I'd say come in for a drink,' Walter suddenly said. 'I can go to Oddbins any time.'

'Or I could walk there with you,' said Annie, without knowing why. Perhaps she just didn't want to stand there on the pavement in the cold any longer.

So they set off together. Walter wasn't under any illusions. He realised he was falling in love with Annie and he felt happy. They walked fast and either that or his own emotion made him forget the cold. Walter hadn't fallen in love for years; in fact he hadn't really expected to do so again.

In Oddbins they bumped into Sarah's husband, Neil, buying gin and bottles of tonic.

'Must fly,' he said, 'got some people coming to supper. Friends of Sarah's.' But he looked quite surprised, Annie thought, as he made for the door, weighed down by his purchases.

Annie walked back with Walter and, glad to postpone further confrontation with Tamsin, she willingly agreed to have a quick drink with him. Just one glass of wine.

It was the first time Annie had ever been inside Walter's house and she was curious to know what it would be like. In fact it was rather impersonal; pale paint on the walls, dullish colours all around, books all neatly arranged in their shelves, nothing lying about, pretty furniture, quiet

76

and tasteful. The pictures on the wall were mostly old-fashioned prints of plants or insects or birds. She even wondered if the large one over the fireplace of a pair of snow buntings weren't an Audubon.

A baby grand at the far end made the room seem much smaller than Annie's equivalent on the other side of the street. The only sign of disorder anywhere was on the piano where sheet music lay in scattered untidy piles.

'You play the piano?' Annie sounded a little surprised. 'What do you play?'

'Oh, this and that – mostly classical.' Walter was always a little embarrassed when people asked him about his music.

Glancing at the piano, Annie noticed a Bach fugue propped open above the keyboard.

'You haven't said anything about Fred,' Walter remarked, as he pulled the cork from a bottle of wine.

'Fred? Who's Fred?' Annie asked, but as she did so she suddenly noticed an extraordinary creature lying still as a log under the window at the back of the room. 'What on earth is that?' she enquired, amazed.

'That's Fred, of course,' said Walter. 'He's an iguana. I've had him for a long time now. He must be about five or six years old. The only trouble is that he's getting rather large. He's already about two foot six long but they can grow to five foot. If he does get much bigger I'll have to give him away – to a zoo or something. I won't be able to keep him here.'

Annie had never heard of anyone keeping an iguana as a pet and wondered if Fred was attached to Walter.

'Afraid not,' said Walter. 'It's all the other way round. His brain's too small.'

Annie took the glass of wine Walter held out for her and advanced gingerly towards the strange primaeval creature reclining beneath the window. It neither moved nor blinked and she couldn't decide whether she was disgusted or attracted by it, whether it was beautiful or quite the most hideous thing she had ever seen.

'Beauty is in the eye of the beholder,' Walter remarked as if reading her thoughts. 'To me he's beautiful,' he added, as he bent to scratch the strange beast under his scaly chin.

Fred appeared to like the attention he was getting; he raised his head slowly and, pressing down with his forefeet, stiffened his legs, pushing the front of his body off the ground as if luxuriating in the caress. He almost seemed to be smiling.

'Doesn't he make an awful mess?' Annie glanced around anxiously.

'Not really. He usually lives in here.' Walter pointed to a large, glass-sided cage which was partly hidden from sight by the piano. 'He sleeps and eats in there – and he's got his sun lamp in there and all his things, but I let him out sometimes to stretch his legs. He looks pretty clumsy on the floor but you should see him when he climbs the curtains. He's very graceful then.'

Annie looked around at the faded print curtains, relics from Walter's parental home, and wondered that they weren't in shreds. She wasn't sure how much she liked the idea of an iguana climbing up and down curtains but she liked Walter's matter-of-fact attitude to Fred which seemed to be based on some kind of mutual respect. If Fred's cage was anything to go by, with its clean wood shavings, bowls of fresh chopped vegetables and branch of a small tree, then he was well looked after indeed.

'He's company of sorts,' said Walter. 'Have some more wine.'

Annie wanted to stay. She sort of wanted to see Fred shinning up the curtains or returning to his branch to sunbathe under the lamp, but he had settled back into his former position of unblinking immobility under the window. She would also have liked to hear Walter play the piano but she was too shy to ask and in any case she felt he might not have liked it. In fact she knew that she must go as Tamsin would be waiting for supper. Perhaps Annie would even be able to initiate some kind of friendly intercourse with her.

'It was lovely to get out for a moment,' she said as she left. 'I'll have to think about Fred though. Do you think he likes music?'

Walter laughed as he stood on the front doorstep.

Nice laugh, she thought, and nice shirt too for that matter. Funny tie. 'Thanks a lot,' she said. 'See you on Saturday.'

She walked slowly back across the foggy street, deep in thought about Walter and reluctant to re-enter her own world.

When Tamsin came down to supper, it was obvious to Annie that she had been crying. It annoyed Annie to think that she might have been crying about anything so spoilt as a second telephone line, but she said nothing. Besides, some instinct told her that whatever it was that was upsetting Tamsin was nothing quite so trivial. Annie decided to make no enquiries, but she treated her daughter gently and they had a peaceful supper, talking about nothing very much, but by the end of which Annie felt that perhaps some tiny breach had been made in the mighty wall of their misunderstanding.

As they said good-night to one another, Annie looked at her grand and beautiful child and her heart ached at the thought of the unexplained turmoil which must be going on inside. For a moment she even allowed herself to wonder if it was possible that there might be some truth in the revolting rumour about Henry. But the thought, she decided, was un unworthy one and she put it away from her.

Tamsin walked, heavy hearted, up the stairs. At supper she had very nearly decided to talk to her mother about the chat line. She knew she was in trouble there and Annie had seemed to be so kind and gentle and ordinary this evening, yet Tamsin was sure that she wouldn't begin to understand. She'd probably only disapprove. The trouble with Annie was that she was just so old-fashioned and she had no idea of what it was like to be young.

The next day Annie didn't have to go to work, and in the middle of the morning happened to be standing in her bedroom, looking vaguely out of the window and thinking of nothing very much, when she saw Patrick coming out of his house on the opposite side of the street, holding something which looked like a piece of paper in his hand. He had a purposeful, bossy manner about him as he stepped onto the pavement and turned his head, bird-like, from side to side before crossing the road.

Of all the people in the street, Patrick was the one whose company Annie most sought to avoid.

Patrick was a middle-aged bachelor, some kind of business consultant who never seemed to go to an office, a busybody and an active Liberal Democrat. Enough to turn anyone away from the road of moderation. Annie thought of him in his cosy Notting Hill cottage, feeling so passionate about hunting in the shires and about bombing the Serbs. Always buttonholing everybody. He was also the biggest gossip in the neighbourhood. If anything was ever known to have happened to anyone in the street — a bereavement, a birth, an illness, a redundancy — you could be sure that Patrick would always be there, hanging around, waiting to pick up some tidbit. When Isabel's husband had hanged himself in the next street, Patrick had been there too, just happening to pass, head darting from side to side, more than ever like a bird – a bird of prey – just as the corpse was bundled out of the house into the waiting hearse.

Annie was hardly pleased to see that Patrick appeared to be heading straight for her door. He usually came to call when he had some particularly aggravating information to impart. He had, too, an odious habit of cutting little snippets out of the paper which he thought might 'amuse' you. The last one Annie had received, pushed through her letter-box when she was out, had been about the increased risks to foreign correspondents in the former Jugoslavia. Needless to say, Isabel, after her tragedy, had been bombarded with cuttings about suicide, the incidence of male suicide in the thirty-five–fifty age group, how to recognise the danger signs and how to come to terms with your own guilt. As she saw Patrick step up to her front door, Annie wondered what in God's name he had in store for her this morning. She wondered, too, whether or not to bother to open the door to him.

But she needn't have worried. Patrick didn't ring the bell but she heard something drop through the letter-box, and then she watched as he strode off again down the road in his lemon-coloured corduroys and trainers, silver hair blow-dried, elbows out, head held high, turning as ever from side to side – this time as if to acknowledge cheers from bystanders, had there been any.

Annie went downstairs and irritably picked up the envelope which lay on the mat just outside the door. A note written in neat italic hand with obtrusively elaborate capitals was stapled to a newspaper cutting and read, 'I thought this might be of interest. Don't acknowledge but Read and Destroy. Patrick.' Annie glanced at the cutting before crumpling it angrily in her hand. The headline was more than enough for her: 'Child sex abuse knows no social bounds say experts.'

'Sarah. How are you?'

'Oh, Camilla, hello. I'm fine really. Much better. I don't think I'm dying of a brain tumour any more.'

'Thank heavens for that. I had to ring you though – well obviously I wanted to know how you were, but I wondered if you'd heard what I've heard?'

'What've you heard that's new?'

'I've been told, please don't pass it on, I mean, promise you won't tell anyone . . .'

'Of course not. You know me – I won't say a thing. But what is it?'

'Well this is really going to surprise you. It appears that Angie is leaving Henry.'

'Angie leaving Henry?'

'I know. It's amazing, isn't it? But you see, she's always been a bit of a bitch and now that Henry's lost all his money in Lloyd's and he's going to have to sell that house, she's not interested.'

'I wonder if Annie knows.'

'I don't know, but I wouldn't tell her if I were you. It might upset her.'

'I can't see why she should mind; anyway she's bound to tell me as soon as she does know. So what about all that fuss over the annulment?'

'It's ridiculous, isn't it?'

'Henry'll just have to get another one, I suppose – if he wants to marry again. By the way, Neil saw Annie and Walter together in Oddbins last night. What about that?'

'I dunno. Perhaps they just bumped into each other on the way there. They do live in the same street, you know.'

'I suppose so. I hadn't thought of that.'

'Fanny? Camilla.'

'Hi, Camilla.'

'I was just wondering – do you think – I mean it's a bit ridiculous, but I just wondered if that man who Annie was lunching with might conceivably have been Walter?'

'Walter! Don't be ridiculous. I thought you said that the man in the restaurant was incredibly good–looking.'

'Well, I did, but you know how people exaggerate.'

'I know they do, but you wouldn't honestly describe Walter as "incredibly good-looking", now would you?'

'No. But he's perfectly nice looking.'

'He's all right, but nobody would say he was "incredibly good-looking". In any case, I'd hardly think he'd be Annie's type.'

'Probably not, but do you know, Sarah told me that Neil had seen Annie and Walter together the other evening – last night, I think.'

'Sarah's so jealous. She's jealous of Annie and Will, and as for Walter, she thinks he's her property or something.'

'I know. Funny, isn't it?'

'Anyway, I thought Walter was supposed to be having an affair with Isabel.'

'Isabel's a dark horse.'

'So's Walter, come to that. But I must go now; I'll give you a ring this evening. India's worried about Tamsin you know. She says Tamsin's never at school. She must really be worried I think – you see she wouldn't usually say anything to me about Tamsin, in case I said something to Annie – perhaps I should.'

'What's it all about?'

'Tell you another time. I must go now – 'bye.'

VI

Tamsin felt that she was getting into more and more trouble at school and that it was becoming increasingly difficult for her to sidestep that trouble. She knew, and had known for a long time, that there came a point at which the overworked staff gave up on truancy. It was as though they felt that at some stage there was nothing more they could do about it anyway, and then their attitude seemed quite simply to be one of 'It's your own look-out if you don't take the opportunities given to you'. So they would begin to turn a blind eye on any pupil who had gone beyond certain limits and who appeared to be quite unwilling to make any attempt to help him or herself; they gave their attention instead to the eager hard-workers and forgot the rest. But then there came a further stage of truancy and insubordination which could not be ignored. Tamsin feared that this was the stage she was reaching.

There had been a time, though, as she had begun to slack and her attendance had started to decline, when she had been repeatedly hauled over the coals and warned about a future without qualifications. She had been told that she would regret it in later life if she didn't do her chemistry homework, or make more of an effort to jump the wooden horse in the gym or to learn French which, she arrogantly supposed, she would be able to do easily any time, if she felt like it. She had, of course, been told that she was letting down her parents, the school and, worst of all, herself. The next step could well be expulsion and strangely enough Tamsin had no desire whatsoever to be expelled. She dreaded the upheaval that that would cause and she knew that then she would only be sent to another school which might well be far more unpleasant than the one at which she now was. Besides, she liked being where her friends were.

Everything, she felt, had been brought to a head by that silly story about an onion. It had seemed like a perfect excuse at the time. Unflawed. Seamless. Of course she had never dreamed that her cow of a form teacher would start asking for builders' receipts. In fact she thought it the most awful cheek. What right had she to go poking her nose into other people's private lives and asking about their bills and wanting to know which builders they used? It was none of her business. But still the problem remained. Where on earth was Tamsin to get a bona fide looking receipt from? The first few times she was reminded of it she lied and said that she had forgotten to ask her mother; after that she said that her mother had never been sent a receipt, or that she had thrown it away. The teacher merely persisted: Tamsin would have to ask for another copy.

In addition to this annoying problem about the builder's receipt which was permanently niggling at Tamsin – making her sweat and panic in the small hours – there was the problem of how to account for all the extra mornings she was taking off school to work the chat line. In any case, she loathed the chat line, rued the day she had agreed to do it and longed to give it up. The only trouble was that she hadn't as yet received any payment and she felt sure that if she gave up, she would never get a penny out of Dirk. She hated Dirk and didn't trust him and she knew that he had a hold over her in that he could continue to switch the line through to her home to prevent her resigning. This was a sure and safe way of keeping her on the job.

Tamsin's instinctive misgivings about the chat line had proved to be more than well-founded. The anonymous voices of the telephone onanists revolted her. She felt used, abused and degraded as they invited her to participate in their tedious, repetitive and often violent fantasies. Now she had nightmares about rape and blood in which huge monstrous, faceless men threatened her from every side, jumping at her from darkened doorways, lying in wait for her at home, ready to tear her limb from limb, to trample on her, to suffocate her.

She didn't know what on earth to do. She dared not tell her mother and she hesitated to tell her best friend, Susie, because Susie's other best friend was Isabel's daughter and Isabel was quite a friend of Annie's. Annie's friends gossiped and Tamsin did not want to be gossiped about by anyone, least of all by her mother's friends. She tried to confide in Billy but Billy just moved his shoulders, stuck out his chin, took hold of his pony-tail, ran it through his hand and said, 'Don't take it all so seriously, Tams. There's no need to get so worked up.'

Neither was Billy at all helpful when Tamsin asked him when she might expect to get paid. He told her she'd just have to be patient. If she still hadn't been paid in a week's time, he'd consider giving Dirk a ring. Or Tamsin could always give him a ring herself. Tamsin wasn't wet and she'd already tried that a few times but Dirk lived beyond an answer phone.

Tamsin was someone who held two opposing views of herself. Sometimes she saw herself as a complete and utter failure, no good at anything, liked by no one, gauche, gangling and large, who had fallen in with Billy, a bad lot, and who therefore deserved everything that was coming to her. At other times she thought she was tall and glamorous, better looking than her friends, smarter and more sophisticated and pretty clever. When she was in this more optimistic frame of mind, she believed that the world was at her feet and that even now, if she set to work in time, she was clever enough still to pass her exams with a certain amount of success. She had worked out that 'in time' probably meant by the Easter holidays. Because she quite rightly believed herself to be clever, Tamsin could not contemplate with any degree of equanimity the prospect of failing her exams entirely, yet now she had reached a point where to open a book reminded her of all the work undone and so produced in her some kind of blind panic which caused her immediately to close the book again and to tell herself that the Easter holidays would be time enough.

As she walked back from school, dragging her feet rather, and seeing herself this afternoon as a gauche failure, a hopelessly inadequate fool, Tamsin was feeling close to tears. How the hell was she to sort out all these muddles? Whichever way she looked there seemed to be trouble. She sensed the presence of someone beside her and turned to see India falling into step with her. India's mother was Fanny – another friend, or at least acquaintance, of Annie's.

'Hi!' said India.

'Hi,' Tamsin replied disconsolately. India wasn't a particular friend of hers and she didn't especially want to talk to her at the moment.

India was small and jolly and good at her books and didn't play truant, and she had all the right ideas and was a very decent sort. India's mother was very pleased indeed with India because India worked well and had sensible friends and wanted to go to university and agreed with her mother about drugs and not sleeping with boys. In fact India was beginning to disagree with her mother on this latter point but she hadn't yet shared her changed views with Fanny. She was waiting to see what happened – there was this really nice boy in her physics class . . .

Like her friends, India was sensible, and she was kind too. She believed her own attitude to the world to be pre-eminently wise and grown-up and she liked the role of confidante and adviser to her peers. It was a role to which she felt herself to be perfectly suited because she was such a caring person. She was hoping to do her degree in psychology and then to go on to do some kind of counselling. Fanny was proud of her daughter's ambition.

'You okay Tamsin?' India gently probed as the two girls continued walking side by side.

'Fine,' said Tamsin, tossing her head and blinking back a tear. She wished India would shut up – go away – she didn't want India's sympathy.

'It's just that you don't look very happy these days and people are wondering what the matter is . . .'

'Oh piss off!' said Tamsin, and burst into tears.

India turned her round face towards Tamsin's and looked earnestly up at her. She tried to put her arms round her but was hampered by the school bags they both carried and by the fact that Tamsin shrugged her off roughly.

'I can't just leave you here crying in the street,' said India, genuinely distressed. 'Let's find somewhere where we can have a cup of coffee, then perhaps you'll feel better.'

By this time Tamsin was sobbing helplessly and had so lost control of the situation that, despite her irritation with India, she allowed herself to be led into a café where she sat down at a table, buried her head in both her hands and gave one last shuddering sob before fumbling in her pocket for a cigarette and lighting it while India ordered cups of coffee.

'Would you like to tell me what's the matter?' India's caring face, pushed so eagerly forward, looked rounder than ever to Tamsin through the haze of cigarette smoke. Suddenly Tamsin wanted to laugh – India looked so funny sitting there, with that intense, anxious expression on her baby face.

'Somebody said you wanted to be a doctor,' Tamsin said. 'Is it true? I can't imagine going to a doctor and it being you.'

'Doctors come in all shapes and sizes,' India said a little huffily. 'But actually I'm going to be a counsellor.'

The two girls talked disjointedly for a while about nothing much, and then Tamsin said, 'I say, thanks. You've been jolly nice. It's just that I've got a few problems.' She drew on her cigarette. 'But it'll be okay. I'm fine really.' Tamsin didn't want to enlarge, partly because she wouldn't have known where to start, and partly because she really couldn't imagine telling India, of all people, about the chat line. India would be so shocked. She couldn't even tell her about the builder's receipt because India wouldn't begin to be able to imagine why she had invented the story about the onion in the first place. At the time that story had struck Tamsin as being a stroke of genius, a watertight excuse, but look where that stroke of genius had got her now!

'Is it something about Billy?' India looked so caring and she did so long to hear the tragic details of a romance which could in no way touch her but which, like the theatre or the cinema, might give her a glimpse of the real world – its heartache and its disappointments.

'You don't know Billy, do you?' Tamsin was surprised.

India didn't know Billy, but everyone knew about him and Tamsin had been seen often enough arriving late for school in his low-slung two-seater. Everyone knew he was very good-looking and a lot of girls were jealous of Tamsin because of him, which meant that malicious stories of every kind had been spread indiscriminately throughout the school.

'Anyway, it's nothing to do with Billy,' Tamsin said, although it seemed all at once that everything awful was somehow something to do with Billy and at that very moment she wished that she might never set eyes on him again.

India was disappointed by Tamsin's reluctance to talk, but had decided by now that she really needed help, particularly if what she had heard from her mother about Tamsin and her father was true. It seemed to India that her role was determined – the path before her was clear and she should not hesitate to take it. She felt truly important as she set out to meddle so gratuitously in another person's life.

'Tamsin,' she said gently, 'if you want to talk to me about your father you can, you know. I won't say anything to anyone.'

Tamsin was amazed. 'About Dad? What do I want to talk about Dad for?' No one could have been further from her mind at that moment than Henry.

'Well, I just thought you might want to talk . . .'

Suddenly Tamsin began to perceive something nasty emerging from the fog of her incomprehension, and what she perceived made her feel sick. She couldn't quite grasp what it was though, as the awfulness of what she half understood refused properly to take shape in her mind and the reality of what India was saying eluded her.

'We're all worried about you,' India ploughed on. 'They say you're showing all the signs . . .'

Tamsin's mouth was hanging open. Why didn't India stop talking?

'Mum says that when people are abused, there is a tendency to truancy . . . You ought to tell someone you know, or it could wreck your life. Mum says it could make you frigid for ever and hate men and all that – she says everyone's talking about it and that your mother really ought to get some sort of help for you . . .'

'Why don't you tell your fucking mother to shut up?' Tamsin rose to her feet, knocking over her coffee cup as she did so, snatched up her bag and with a fresh burst of tears, strode out into the street, leaving India still drinking her coffee.

At first India wondered whether she should run out into the street behind her friend but immediately realised that she was prevented from doing so by the fact that they hadn't yet paid. Anyway why should she follow Tamsin when she was angry with her for talking about her mother like that and for making such an exhibition in public? There had been absolutely no need to get so worked up – the people at the next table were still staring at India who smiled at them, put her forefinger to her temple and twisted it round. Then she paid for the coffee and left, flushed with indignation at the treatment she had received when all she had been trying to do was help. Of one thing she was certain. There was not a shadow of doubt in her mind that Tamsin had been – for all she knew, was still now being – abused by her father.

Sarah was feeling more than usually dissatisfied with life. Neil was turning into something of a workaholic who never seemed to be at home any more, Walter was always out when she rang him, Annie seemed to have become rather shirty of late – no doubt because of all the problems which she determinedly refused to discuss with her old friend, Sarah; the weather was foul and life had lost its lustre. There was no food in the house so she was on her way to buy something for supper, and wondering rather miserably whom to get to come and share it with her, when she bumped into Tamsin who was presumably on her way back from school.

As they stopped to exchange a few words, Sarah could not help noticing that Tamsin had been crying. Her tear-stained face was filthy and her eyes quite swollen and red so that she did not look at all her usual glamorous, haughty self. It really was high time somebody did something about the poor child. Sarah couldn't think what Annie was up to.

She attempted a few friendly, if rather half-hearted, overtures but felt herself immediately rebuffed by Tamsin's cool, off-hand replies. As she crossed the Bayswater Road to Nisa's, she felt a sudden, genuine surge of unselfish concern for the girl, but a few moments later, as she wheeled her trolley round the shop and lifted unseasonal mangetouts and Greek yoghurt off the shelves, she returned to her more customary, heartless mode.

When she got home again, she decided to ring Walter at work as she thought that might annoy him a little, and it might also bring herself more forcibly to his attention.

Walter was sorry but he couldn't have supper with Sarah; he was going to spend the evening with a colleague who'd just got back from Dubai where he'd been looking at giant fossil elephants.

'That should be interesting,' Sarah paused to allow the full weight of her scorn to be felt. Then she said, 'I've almost forgotten what you look like, it's been so long since I saw you,' and put the telephone down without waiting for a reply.

She stamped around the kitchen, putting away her shopping angrily and thinking of giant fossil elephants.

She didn't believe a word of it. Walter was just trying to wind her up. Who'd ever heard of giant fossil elephants? And in Dubai? What nonsense! She'd ring Isabel and ask her to supper, then she'd know all she needed to know about giant fossil elephants. Of course that was where Walter was going – round to Isabel's. She hated the way he couldn't tell her the truth. Why should she always be kept in the dark?

To Sarah's amazement – and indeed confusion – Isabel said, yes, she would love to come round and have supper. What a nice idea.

In fact the last thing Isabel wanted to do was to have supper with Sarah, but she had been caught on the hop. As soon as she had put the telephone down, she began to try to think of some genuine-sounding excuse whereby she could ring back and cancel the arrangement, but she couldn't think of anything so she reluctantly decided that the best thing to do would be just to go, and put a brave face on it.

The trouble with Sarah was that she was tricky. You never knew where you were with her nor could you ever exactly guess at her hidden agenda. For a variety of reasons, Sarah was the last person with whom Isabel relished the thought of spending the evening. But then, they had been friends – of sorts – for years. Sarah, Isabel thought, was probably quite unhappy. But then, who, she wondered, among her friends was happy? Annie didn't look very happy and everybody said she was having some kind of nervous breakdown; Fanny, she supposed, might be all right – but then you never could tell.

After the terrible shock of her husband's suicide, Isabel thought that she could never be happy again, but now, at last, she was beginning to regain her composure, so that without being able to describe herself as happy, she might say that she had found some kind of uneasy contentment; but then everything in her life seemed so very uncertain.

The evening proved to be as uncomfortable as Isabel had anticipated. Sarah was clearly in a very resentful frame of mind, discontented, sorry for herself and ready to lay the blame for her woes at anybody's feet but her own. Neil was always away, leaving her to fend for herself and never telling her of his movements. How could she make any arrangements for her own life, if she didn't know whether Neil would be back on Thursday or Friday? Men were so selfish – didn't Isabel agree?

Isabel hated the old song about the selfishness of the male sex in whose chorus she had used so gladly to join. She knew now that to her dying day she would never hear it without a twinge of pain. The guilt would never go; she would always believe that if she had been a little less concerned with her own affairs, she might have noticed the incipient signs of despair in the man she loved and he might have been alive to this day.

'I reckon we're all pretty selfish,' she sighed, 'one way or another.'

Sarah didn't really think she was selfish. But she thought that she might go off her head one of these days because she had to spend so much time alone – already it was doing her no good and none of her friends seemed to care. There was Walter who was being perfectly horrible to her of late – and Walter was a very old friend. 'Perhaps he thinks I gossip about him,' she added darkly.

Suddenly Sarah felt irritated by the presence of Isabel in her kitchen. What was she doing there, giving nothing away? Stealing Walter from under Sarah's nose. Not that Sarah wanted to have an affair with Walter. No, she certainly didn't want that. She would have had one by now, if that was what she had wanted. Or so she told herself. She thought it was awful of Isabel to be having anything to do with Walter anyway. Isabel was the last person Walter needed to get involved with, what with her unhappy past and that haunting suicide in the background. Talk about selfish! In Sarah's view, the most selfish thing anyone could do was to kill themselves, especially if they had a wife and children.

'You'll probably be wanting to go now,' Sarah said abruptly, and stood up. 'It must be dreadfully boring for you just sitting here and listening to me. I'm becoming such a dull person these days.' So Isabel was dismissed at an early hour.

When she had left, Sarah thought again about Walter. What Walter needed was indeed someone more like herself, someone with a bit of understanding – a bit of originality. She decided to ring him again. She'd see about these fossil elephants. Isabel had left remarkably early, no doubt because she had a rendezvous with Walter.

Sarah rang Walter's number. It was answered by an answer machine. She didn't leave a message, but rang off.

Annie desperately wanted to get out of London, if only for a few days. She was fed up with the enclosed atmosphere of the little streets where she lived, where everybody seemed to know everyone else's business and where, recently, the gossip seemed to have grown out of all proportion.

She needed to think carefully about Tamsin's problems and how best to help her deal with them. The school had been in touch with Annie again lately and it appeared that she was practically never there. There was a very real threat that she would be asked to leave before she had even sat her GCSEs. Then there was the problem of what she should do next year. Henry's idea of sending her to a convent school was clearly out of the question.

There was something else beyond the lying and the

truancy which was worrying Annie about her daughter, but she simply couldn't think what lay behind it.

Annie had not gone into work one morning because her students were sitting an exam and Tamsin had behaved in a most peculiar fashion. Tamsin should have been going to school and had indeed looked as if that was her intention until the moment when Annie had said casually that she was staying at home herself. Annie could only see Tamsin's behaviour at that moment in terms of panic. Why had Tamsin been so desperate to get her mother out of the house if she herself had been planning to go to school? She had begun to make the most ludicrous suggestions all of which involved Annie going out.

'You need a new winter coat,' Tamsin had almost screamed. 'You can't go around in that awful old thing any longer. You look a mess. Why don't you go out and get one?'

In February, when the winter was three-quarters done? In any case, with their usual disregard for season, the shops were already full of T-shirts and bikinis.

Annie wondered to what she owed this sudden, unprecedented attack on her winter coat and firmly decided not to budge.

The next thing that happened was that Tamsin was struck – apparently quite out of the blue – by the most appalling migraine headache. Tamsin was an excellent, if histrionic actress, and an outsider might well have had no difficulty in believing the wretched girl to be suffering from the acutest and most debilitating pain. But Annie had her doubts. Still, she could not, with an entirely clear conscience, insist on sending her off to school. So Tamsin stayed at home and, to Annie's amazement, and despite her terrible migraine, she spent half the morning on the telephone, having leapt to answer it before Annie whenever it rang.

Annie was not in the habit of eavesdropping on her daughter's telephone conversations but she did notice that whenever she went into the sitting-room where Tamsin was crouched secretively over the telephone, a peculiarly uncomfortable atmosphere pervaded and Tamsin appeared to clam up. What on earth, Annie wondered, was going on?

By midday, Tamsin seemed to have calmed down somewhat and when Sarah rang a little later, Annie was able to answer the telephone herself.

'I couldn't remember if today was one of those days you go to work,' Sarah said. 'But it's obviously not. I've been ringing you all morning and the line's been permanently engaged. Lucky you to have so many friends . . .'

Annie was irritated. She turned, only half listening to Sarah's whingeing, and looked at Tamsin slouching on the sofa.

Caught like that, unawares, Tamsin looked dreadful, tired and heavy and colourless and utterly unhappy. Annie felt a knife turn in her heart. Perhaps if she took her daughter away for a few days she would be able to get her to talk about what it was that was troubling her so. If Annie didn't know what the matter was, she could do nothing to help. Suddenly she felt a surge of rage against Henry. If he had laid a finger on that girl, she would kill him . . .

'Are you still there?' She heard Sarah's voice down the telephone. 'I thought we must have been cut off, but you weren't listening. Oh, I know, everybody thinks I've become so dull these days – even Isabel who came round last night could hardly get out of the door fast enough as soon as we'd finished supper – and as for Walter, I absolutely never see him any more . . .'

'Oh, Sarah, for Christ's sake!' Annie suddenly felt herself snap.

Sarah slammed down the telephone. Annie merely sighed and quietly replaced the handset. *Raison de plus* for getting out of London. Sarah.

'I don't know why you have anything to do with that frightful woman,' Tamsin said in a dull voice without looking up.

'Oh, she's all right,' said Annie. 'She's just lonely and not very happy. Anyway, she's an old friend.'

'No wonder she's unhappy,' Tamsin remarked. 'All she ever does is to have dinner parties and gossip and go shopping. Why doesn't she get a job or climb a mountain or go abseiling, or even work in a charity shop. Find some interest in life.' Tamsin spoke with sudden feeling. She had a tendency to think that everyone else's problems were far more easily solved than her own and was therefore somewhat impatient of them.

'Life's more complicated than that,' said Annie. 'So, who was that you were talking to all the morning on the telephone?'

'Oh, nobody,' Tamsin replied. Then added, 'Just somebody . . .' and left it at that. She wished she could tell her mother that she had been listening to – and conniving in – the most disgusting, pointless rigmarole she had ever imagined, while some inadequate jerk tossed himself off at the other end of the line, and that she felt guilty and cheap, used and abused – almost as if she had been raped. At that moment she hated the entire male sex, but most of all she hated herself.

'If your headache's better,' said Annie, 'why don't we go round the corner to the pub for some lunch – cheer ourselves up. Then you can go on to school. I'll give you a note.'

Tamsin could have hugged her mother who, she

sometimes thought, was the nicest person on earth, but she just said, with a wry smile, 'Life's more complicated than that, Mum. Anyway, I don't feel very well. I think I'll go to bed.'

Annie said she'd give herself some bread and cheese and then ring Sarah and go round and see her, if she was in. She was feeling rather bad about Sarah.

'Apparently she came round to supper, swallowed her food and bolted out of the door. That's not very friendly, is it? Quite frankly, I'm on Sarah's side over this.'

'Well, you've only heard Sarah's side of the story.'

'I know, but honestly, Camilla, you don't do that, I mean do you? She didn't even finish her coffee, she was in such a tearing hurry to get back to Walter who, according to Sarah, had made some totally improbable excuse for not being around. Something about going to look for dinosaurs in Dublin. Really! Couldn't he have thought of something a bit more convincing? I don't blame Sarah for feeling hurt.'

'All I can say is that I saw Isabel this morning, who asked me if I'd seen Sarah lately. She thought Sarah was in a rather bad way and, to tell you the truth, I was quite surprised by how concerned she seemed. Anyway, she told me she'd been round there last night and had a very good supper, and then Sarah suddenly sort of dismissed her.'

'I don't believe that. You don't suddenly dismiss people. Isabel was obviously feeling guilty about rushing away like that, and she was probably worried about what Sarah was going to say about it to us, so she invented that. If she behaved as badly as she obviously did, she would want to get her version of events round first, wouldn't she?'

'Fanny, I've never known you to be so tough.'

'Well I have just been talking to Sarah, and I couldn't help feeling sorry for her. Neil leaves her alone an awful lot, you know.'

'I know – and she's very attractive. Perhaps she's up to something.'

'No – I think we'd know.'

'So – what's the news about Tamsin? Have you heard anything more from India?'

'Well, yes. It is rather awful actually. You really mustn't tell this to anyone, will you? I mean, it would be too dreadful – and of course, I did swear to India that I wouldn't tell a soul.'

'Oh now, Fanny, would I?'

'No, of course, I know you wouldn't. India's such a kind person, you see – she's been really worried about Tamsin – and it's not as if those two were great friends. They've known each other always, of course, but then they're quite different types. India's always wanted to work – thank God – and then she's not interested in boys. She gets on with them all right. She's got lots of friends who are boys – but she's terribly sensible. I know we're awfully lucky. But where was I? Oh yes, Tamsin. So India had a heart-to-heart with her the other day – they all pour their hearts out to India – and – well, it does appear that it is true. About Henry.'

'And she told India?'

'Yes. She did.'

'How awful! What did poor India do?'

'India was dreadfully upset. She had to talk to me about it. She couldn't have kept a thing like that to herself.'

'What are you going to do about it?'

'I've no idea. What do you think I ought to do?'

'You certainly ought to speak to Annie. Perhaps you ought to go to the police.'

'Do you really think so? I can't do that because I

promised India I wouldn't tell anyone. Oh Lord! Look at the time! We've been on this telephone for over half an hour – I must fly. 'Bye.'

VII

'Sarah, hallo. How are you? It's Camilla.'

'Oh, hallo. I'm all right, I suppose. How are you? I haven't seen you for ages. But then I haven't seen anyone. I think I'm turning into a really dull person.'

'Oh, go on, I'm sure you're not. I saw Isabel just now and she said she'd been round to have supper with you last night. How was she?'

'She was all right – didn't stay a minute – dashed off in a tearing hurry to meet Walter. She didn't have to come to supper, did she? The real trouble with Isabel, of course, is that she's dreadfully selfish. Don't you think so?'

'I certainly think she's changed a lot in the last couple of years. But surely she didn't just leave like that, all of a sudden, without giving you any excuse, did she?'

'She absolutely did. Honestly, Camilla, I was quite hurt. She just ran for the door. I can't think what Walter's done to her. At least she didn't used to be like that. I always thought she was very friendly – the sort of person you could really feel relaxed with and who you could chat to for hours. She never seemed in a hurry.'

'How do you know she was going to meet Walter?'

'She made it perfectly obvious. Besides, what she didn't

know was that I'd rung Walter earlier and he'd invented some cock-and-bull story about wild elephants or something because he didn't want to come round here to supper. I never had any intention of asking Isabel in the first place. It was just that I was so annoyed with Walter that I rang her to see what she was up to and – I dunno – I just asked her to supper. She didn't have to come.'

'I must say, it is rather odd of her to have behaved like that. If she knew she was going to have to dash off, why on earth did she agree to come?'

'I can't think. Anyway, I'm pretty fed up with her.'

'I'm not surprised.'

'I don't understand this thing about Walter at all. After all, she's known him for years without anything coming of it.'

'But I've always thought Isabel was a bit odd – haven't you? The way she reacted to the suicide and all that – and there have been so many stories about her, but she's such a dark horse, you never know what's really going on.'

'I know, but then, there's no smoke without fire.'

'People say she's had all these affairs, but do you think she has?'

'Of course she has. Why would anyone want to invent it?'

'God only knows. Anyway, have you see Annie lately?'

'I'm leaving her alone for a bit. She's in a very bad frame of mind – snaps your head off before you've even had time to open your mouth.'

'Oh.'

'Why?'

'It's just that I thought you might be the one to do something.'

'Do something about what?'

'Well, this Tamsin thing. You know – Tamsin and Henry.'

'What on earth am I supposed to do?'

'Well, listen, Sarah, this really is in confidence. You mustn't tell a soul or I'll be in terrible trouble.'

'Camilla, you must know me by now. I'm incredibly discreet. I never pass anything on and certainly wouldn't dream of discussing something like that with anyone. You know I wouldn't. It could be very dangerous – not to say hurtful.'

'You really won't say a word about this, will you?'

'Don't be silly.'

'You see Fanny absolutely swore me to secrecy. She promised India she wouldn't say anything to anyone herself. What apparently happened was that Tamsin broke down and told India all about it. About Henry – and all that. Just think what the poor girl must be going through.'

'Do you mean it's still really going on?'

'Well – yes. I rather gather it is.'

'How disgusting! I never liked Henry anyway. Did you?'

'I though he was just a bit of a prig, but I've always said – I said it when these rumours started – that Catholic schools can have a very funny effect on some people – men in particular.'

'Oh, I know that. But what is it you want me to do?'

'I thought you could have a word with Annie or something . . .'

Angie had gone to the walled garden to prune the espaliered apple trees that lined the central path. Half-way up the garden a second path intersected the main path, making a little crossroads where a round pond edged with grey coping stones formed a central point of interest. In the middle of the pond an eroded statue of a little putto made a fountain by peeing over the heads of the big, fat goldfish which glided heedlessly by beneath him.

The trees should have been pruned earlier but the weather had been so cold and bleak and bad that Angie, in spite of her real love for the garden, had been discouraged from putting a foot out of doors. It was not the house, or her husband, or even her baby, that Angie really loved, but the garden – and most especially the walled vegetable garden. It held a magic for her – as it did for Tamsin – so that in it she felt protected, almost cocooned, and completely cut off from the anxieties of everyday life. She also felt, as she gardened, as if she were, for once, part of something. Part of a chain of events, or a divine order. She didn't know which and she didn't mind. Perhaps it was important for her to feel part of something which yielded to her and which could neither threaten her in any way nor contradict her for, despite her good looks and confident manner, she was at heart frightened. Frightened of being thought foolish, frightened of not getting it quite right, frightened of not belonging. Frightened, in fact, of her own insignificance.

As a result of all this fear, Angie thought about herself rather a lot and attached a certain amount of importance to what others thought about her, too. But in the garden, alone with the apple trees and the goldfish and the fat little putto, she could forget all this and devote herself to the earth and things that grew. She certainly didn't go to the garden to think, but because she loved the smell of the earth, the pure air and the feeling she had there of creation, or of imposing order on chaos. She loved wheeling a barrow-load of manure, clipping a hedge, hoeing a border. She even loved to see the pink worms squirming as she turned a forkful of clean earth. Nothing in her life was more satisfying.

This morning, as she walked through the garden, she was feeling particularly tense and angry with Henry. The baby she had left with the daily help who was due to go home at twelve. Henry she had left talking on the telephone to his stockbroker. She had just had a dreadful quarrel with him because he had again refused to pay for a nanny, on the grounds that with the losses he had sustained at Lloyd's, he was in no position to afford such a luxury. Angie did not consider a nanny to be a luxury, and neither, generally speaking, did she take Henry's losses seriously.

Even had he felt that he could afford a nanny, Henry would have been reluctant to do so. In his antiquated view of the world, women who, lucky things, had been formed from Adam's rib, were created as helpmeets for their men, and to bear fruit. Theirs, he craftily argued, was a privileged role in which they succoured the teeming human race. All their creativity was spent in the act of parturition and in the subsequent years of bottom-washing, nose-wiping and listening to the first incoherent attempts at reading. With work like this to do, how could women expect to write books, paint pictures, compose symphonies – or still less, go out to work in a bank or an office? Women who did these things were, he thought, not only denying their own creativity, but also denying the Great Design. One of the things which, Henry thought, had really come between himself and Annie, had been her insistence on going out to work. Angie, he felt, should look after her son herself or there would be trouble brewing. Henry blamed all Tamsin's problems on Annie's denial of the Great Design.

A bright, wintry sun was shining, promising the approach of spring, so that Angie felt her anger and irritation quickly ebb as she entered her magic world and closed the garden door behind her. A group of primroses nestled by the wall, daring so early in the year to open their delicate faces and turn them to the elements.

Angie would have hated to leave this garden and could

not imagine what would happen if Henry ever had to sell the house, but whenever she approached him about his financial affairs, he invariably refused to discuss them, so that in fact she had no idea to what degree, if at all, her present way of life was threatened; and for the most part she refused to dwell on the matter.

Now, riled by Henry's talk of affording and not affording, she allowed herself for a moment to speculate. If they did sell, where would they move to? Certainly to nowhere with such a beautiful walled garden. Sometimes Angie went so far as to think that the walled gaden was all that now tied her to Henry. Having won the bitter battle to wrest him from Annie, she could not but think that the salt had lost its savour, and sometimes she even wondered at Annie for having so desperately wanted to keep him. How, she asked herself, had Annie dealt with all the bigoted Catholicism, not to mention Henry's pitiable attitude to women? Neither of those things had bothered her at first. In the early days, she'd laughed them aside and thought only of winning the battle and getting what she wanted.

If Angie ever really had to leave this garden, she thought, as she walked in the sunshine up the path between the apple trees, she might well seek new pastures and leave Henry altogether. She didn't know what he would do for an annulment this time. Not that he'd need one from her, she thought, he could just declare the first one to be the bunch of lies it was and start again from scratch. For herself, she wouldn't care although, of course, if Henry's annulment was invalid, then she had never been married in the eyes of God anyway. She snorted at the thought of God and at the folly of it all.

When Angie returned to the house, she felt elated by two hours of solitary pruning and satisfied with her work so that her anger with Henry had temporarily evaporated.

She opened the fridge, looking for something to have for lunch and took out a jar of puréed boeuf bourguignon and carrots for Matthew; there didn't seem to be much for her and Henry. She was just thinking that she would probably be able to find a pizza in the deep freeze, when Henry came into the kitchen, shoulders hunched, tense, and visibly annoyed.

He'd had a bad morning on the telephone to various men of affairs and he was beginning to wonder where he was going to turn for money next. He had made a fortune in refuse collection before selling out a few years earlier, since when he had grown quite accustomed to living off the fat of the land. It was then, in those heady, moneyed days that he'd semi-retired and bought the house with the walled garden. Now he still had a finger in one or two pies which took him to London a couple of days a week.

Rather than sell the house – that would be the last thing to go – he might sell the flat in London. He wouldn't miss it very much, but still he hated the idea of having to sell something which he had regarded as an excellent invest- ment. He didn't want to tell Angie about his problems, partly because he kept hoping that he'd be able to find some way round them without having to sell, and partly because he was a little afraid of what her reaction might be.

Henry loved Angie but he was a million miles away from understanding her. It never occurred to him that with such a blinkered view of the world – and of women in particular – as he had, his chances of understanding the human heart were somewhat limited. When Angie was cold to him, which he had noticed her being increasingly of late, he merely concluded that all women were moody. She should be happy, he thought, for she had no financial worries, everything she needed – a lovely house, friends, holidays abroad and a baby. He even added a perfectly nice husband to that list.

Henry glanced absent-mindedly at Angie, his shoulders still hunched. He didn't like the way women these days were always wearing trousers, but he had to admit that his wife, with her long legs, looked good in jeans. She had spent the morning in the garden, he knew, so he presumed that would have put her in a good mood. When he had last seen her, after breakfast, she had been quite sarcastic to him – something about wanting a nanny. He couldn't see why she wanted a nanny; after all, she had nothing else to do but to look after Matthew – but then women were so illogical.

'I'm just going to put a pizza in the oven for our lunch,' she said. She was holding a large, frozen one in her hand. A moment later she left the room to fetch Matthew who'd been having his morning sleep and was now due for his boeuf bourguignon.

Henry sat down at the table and allowed himself to think for a moment about his son. He was glad he was a boy. He'd probably be good at chess and reasonable, as well. Quite unlike Tamsin who was beautiful and unreasonable – in fact impossible. He couldn't understand why Annie was so adamantly against sending her to a convent when it was quite obviously the answer for the moment to her problems. That was another worry, though, because he wasn't quite sure how he was going to be able to pay for it if she did go.

Henry always thought he had a strong nerve and a lot of nous, but suddenly, as he buried his face in his hands and took a deep breath which more closely resembled a sigh, he began to feel that everything was getting on top of him. Perhaps he'd go round after lunch to see if Father Leatham was in. He always felt better after a session with Father

Leatham. Probably because the priest flattered him, bolstered up his prejudices and condoned his bigotry.

Just as Angie came back with Matthew who was crying and whining from cold and general irritation at having just woken up, the telephone rang.

Henry rose wearily to his feet and said, 'I'll get it.'

'Hi, Dad, it's Tamsin,' came his daughter's voice. 'I thought I'd like to come down this weekend. Are you going to be at home?'

'Of course.' Henry's heart sank at the prospect of Angie's cold reception of the news. She had been very sarcastic about Tamsin since the last visit and had even expressed the hope that she wouldn't come again for some time.

When Henry had remarked that his house was a home for his daughter, Angie had snapped that it certainly was not.

'I'll be on the usual train,' said Tamsin, and then added rather ominously, 'I want to talk to you.'

Henry felt the world closing in on him.

'I don't think I'll have any lunch,' he said. 'I have to go and see Father Leatham.'

As he walked through the village to the ugly little modern bungalow where the priest lived, Henry's heart felt somewhat lighter. Father Leatham had helped him through so many crises of conscience, as, for instance, when Angie had let it be known that she intended to continue to take the pill. Secretly, with all his money problems, Henry didn't want any more children, but another part of him thought that Angie was doing wrong and that, in any case, it was her duty to multiply and bring forth. Father Leatham had made it all all right by pointing out that Henry need know nothing of what Angie was doing and that in any case the sin was with her. Henry's conscience was clear. As clear as the conscience of a

Catholic man married to a Protestant wife. It was very convenient. Convenient, Henry thought, but quickly eclipsed the concept from his mind. Perhaps Father Leatham would have some further words of comfort to offer where Tamsin was concerned.

Annie had heard from Will that he would be home in a few weeks. He didn't give her the exact date, but it wouldn't be long now. On the telephone he had sounded tense and exhausted, yet, as he rang off, Annie was rather shocked to realise that instead of the usual feeling of excitement and joy with which she greeted news of his homecoming, she sensed an inexplicable anticlimax.

She wondered about it for a while, and felt guilty. When she tried to rationalise it, she decided that it must be due to the fact that he had been away too long this time so that they were more out of touch than usual. Besides, she had shared none of her troubles with him, troubles which of late had so occupied her mind. It was as though Will's return this time would be more of an effort for her. After the tough times he had been through and all the horrors he must have experienced, it was her duty to put him first, or so she felt. He should be welcomed, cosseted, made comfortable in every possible way before he set off again for God knows where – Rwanda perhaps. Her own infinitely parochial worries and her loneliness must be set to one side, but after the long, grey winter, she felt almost too weary to make the effort. In a moment of self-pity, she just wished that someone would occasionally cosset her, but then she quickly reminded herself of how lucky she was not to be a Bosnian Muslim.

With a sigh, she turned her attention back to the English exercises she was correcting. She was beginning to find the job a little tedious and to be irritated by the lack of interest in language displayed by so many of her students. They seemed to think that you could pour the English language – or any other for that matter – from some gigantic jug through a funnel into their brains while they passively received it. It never seemed to occur to so many of them that to succeed they had to grapple with the language, use their ears to listen to it and their eyes to read it on every possible occasion, that they needed to be amused and intrigued by it and that, above all, they needed some glimmer of understanding of the philosophy of grammar. She was sick to death of their elementary mistakes, of reading 'she don't' and 'I am having one sister and three brothers'.

'Oh, boo!' she said out loud to herself, and sighed again. She wished she hadn't left her old job, especially since it didn't seem to have made any difference to Tamsin, her being at home more often.

She stood up and stretched and decided to go upstairs and fetch another jersey, not that she was particularly cold, but she had reached the point where any interruption to her work was welcome.

In her bedroom she idly looked out of the window and saw Patrick on the pavement opposite, deep in conversation with Sarah. She wondered what pernicious brew they were concocting, and wondered, too, if Sarah was on her way to call.

Patrick's face, flushed like a turkey-cock's, was pushed forward into Sarah's, his head on one side, spitting, Annie felt sure, as he emphasised all the most thrilling details of someone else's tragedy. He had a couple of books clasped under his left arm whilst with his right hand he gesticulated wildly. So much so that his arm must have ached, or perhaps the books were heavier than they looked, but as Annie watched, he suddenly interrupted the flow to move the books to the right-hand side, thus freeing the left hand for further gesticulation.

Sarah looked quite interested in whatever it was that Patrick had to say, and showed no sign of wanting to move on. Annie wondered how she could stick the man. Sarah could be tricky, but she was a friend and as such, or so it seemed to Annie, she ought to be above being drawn into the slurry of Patrick's mind. Patrick lived and breathed gossip; he lived and breathed other people's misfortunes; if he could, he wormed confidences out of the unsuspecting so as to pass on with greedy, censorious delight, the intimate details of their private lives, whilst pretending all the time to be so caring.

I suppose we all do it, Annie thought, as she turned to go back downstairs to her work, wondering if it would be interrupted again in a minute by Sarah ringing the doorbell to relay Patrick's latest poison. But the more Annie thought about the gossip, the more indefensible she found it to be. Those who indulged in it to any great extent denied that they did or defended it as being an amusing and harmless way of passing the time. No one paid any attention to it, they said. But, if no one was interested, why on earth were so many tidbits of inaccurate information passed around?

Gossips, Annie felt, had something in common with people who turned out to witness public executions. There was always an element of *schadenfreude*, or at least of the heat being on someone other than oneself, and there was also an element of excitement about what would happen next. Who would have egg on their face? Or who would dare do what we would never dare do ourselves, or, worse still, what we would never dream of doing in our morally superior way? There was hardly the slightest piece of gossip, Annie suddenly thought, which did not demean its purveyor, as with glinting eye he or she recounted a neighbour's sexual transgression, bankruptcy or other pitiful misfortune.

Suddenly the bell rang and Annie was brought back to herself. She went to the door and there, sure enough, was Sarah, fresh from her encounter with Patrick.

'You know that big, red-headed man who used to clean windows round here?' Sarah began before she had hardly said hallo or, at Annie's invitation, crossed the threshold.

'What about him?'

'Well, I've just bumped into Patrick and he was telling me that that man has gone to prison for beating up his wife. I thought I hadn't seen him around for a long time. Apparently the wife has got such bad spinal injuries that she's been in hospital for three months and there doesn't seem to be much likelihood of her getting any better.'

'Oh, God,' said Annie. 'How horrible! How does Patrick come to know about all that?'

'Oh, I don't know. He makes it his business to know everything, doesn't he? I think he said the milkman told him.'

'Come and have some coffee,' said Annie, heading for the kitchen, then added rather sharply, 'I wonder who told the milkman.'

'How should I know? They probably live in the same street,' Sarah said irritably, having failed to detect Annie's irony.

They sat at the kitchen table with their cups of coffee. Annie wondered what in particular had brought Sarah, or had she just come for a chat because she was bored, as she used to do before she suddenly became so touchy over the last few months.

'I was just thinking about gossip,' said Annie. 'I'm fed up with it. You can't put your nose out of your own front door around here without number fourteen telling number twenty-two where you're going. Then Patrick will probably pop up and follow you round the corner to see what you're buying at Boots. I can't stand that man. He must have problems. He's probably into auto-erotic asphyxia if only we knew.'

'I thought you didn't approve of gossip,' said Sarah.

'That's not gossip, it's speculation,' said Annie.

'That's all most gossip is,' said Sarah. 'Anyway, thanks to you, I'll never be able to look at Patrick again without wondering if what you've just said is true.'

'Oh Lord,' sighed Annie, 'that's just the trouble. People always believe the horrible things they hear. Or if they don't, they never really disbelieve them. Around here all our names are muck with each other, thanks to people like Patrick, and Fanny and Camilla who probably ring each other up every day.'

'Don't pay any attention,' said Sarah. She was beginning to feel rather uncomfortable as the real reason for her calling, and hoping to find Annie in and alone, was that she had promised Camilla to try to approach Annie about Tamsin, although she knew it would be difficult. Suddenly it seemed an impossible task since anything she had been told was only hearsay – gossip in fact – and when she came to think of it, no one really knew where the rumour had begun. Not with India. It had been rife for months before India had anything to do with it. Perhaps it started with the milkman or the red-headed window cleaner. Perhaps it wasn't true at all. For the first time Sarah asked herself why she had so easily believed it. More or less believed it. Certainly wanted to believe it. She felt ashamed suddenly and, as she looked at Annie, she remembered what old friends they were and, with a genuine impulse of affection, felt that she didn't want to hurt her. She would leave the subject alone.

'How're you liking the job?' she asked instead.

'It's all right at times, but I get pretty bored at others. They all make the same mistakes over and over again. I won't be able to do it for ever.' Then she said, 'Will's coming home you know. You and Neil must come to supper when he gets back.'

As she spoke the telephone rang.

It was Walter. Annie had been seeing quite a lot of Walter lately and she felt that they were becoming good friends. Just that. Nothing more despite the fact that she had now heard him play the piano and had even seen Fred running up the curtain. But it annoyed her to have Sarah sitting there when he rang. She didn't want Sarah to think that she was on such familiar terms with Walter that he knew exactly which days she worked and which she didn't.

Walter was merely ringing to finalise some plan they had for the weekend. A friend he worked with was a fossil elephant expert who, with his wife, had a cottage in Somerset. Annie had met them at Walter's house and liked them. They must have liked her, too, because they included her in an invitation to stay in Somerset just at the moment when Annie most felt like getting out of London. They had invited Tamsin, too, but Annie didn't think she would come and her own answer must depend to some degree on her daughter. In fact, Tamsin had just announced her intention of going to see Henry, so Annie was in the happy position of being able to go away without worrying.

When he heard that Annie could come, Walter was delighted and therefore quite chatty on the telephone about the arrangements; but because of Sarah's presence, she replied rather distantly, making him feel sad that perhaps she didn't really want to come, or for some reason wasn't looking forward to it as much as he was.

'So who was that?' Sarah asked, as Annie rang off. 'You didn't sound very pleased to talk to them.'

'Oh, just someone . . .' Annie replied, almost guiltily. She didn't quite dare to lie and say, 'No one you know.'

'I can't think what you're worried about,' Sarah said. 'No one knows what you get up to when Will's away.'

'Nothing, I'm afraid,' said Annie. 'Have some more coffee?'

'Thanks.' Sarah pushed her cup across the table towards her friend. 'Fanny says that you've been seen wining and dining with an incredibly handsome man – and no one – absolutely no one has any idea who he might be.'

Annie was genuinely puzzled. She had been seeing Walter who was perfectly nice looking, but surely not an incredibly handsome man. Besides they hadn't exactly been wining and dining together. They'd been to the cinema, to a couple of museums, to Kenwood House, but wining and dining – not really, unless you counted the odd pizzeria and their own houses where they surely hadn't been seen. Annie didn't suspect the fossil elephant man of concerning himself with other people's business.

'It was in Chelsea,' Sarah said provocatively.

'I haven't been to Chelsea for months – certainly not to a restaurant.' She paused, and the light suddenly dawned. 'Except with Henry,' she said. 'I did have lunch with Henry a little while ago – and I suppose some people might describe him as incredibly handsome. Lost on me though.' She even vaguely remembered waving to some half-recognised woman who seemed to know her as she left the restaurant.

Sarah was laughing. 'How disappointing,' she said. 'I thought you had a secret love life.'

'There's gossip for you,' said Annie. 'In its truest form. Fanny and Camilla must be eating their hearts out with curiosity. I'm sorry to disappoint them.' She added the last sentence with a certain amount of feeling.

'Think of the hours they've spent speculating about it,'

said Sarah. 'But think of the fun they've had, too.' She distanced herself from the whole affair, although she had been quite as curious as Fanny and Camilla were to know the truth. It was a shame that the truth turned out to be so uninteresting. 'By the way, have you seen Walter at all?' she asked.

'I saw him the other day,' Annie replied vaguely. 'Why?'

'He's given up on me since he took up with Isabel. I can't think why. Perhaps he's just decided that I'm dull. I sometimes think I am.' Sarah was back in her usual groove.

'And, by the way, Camilla, do you remember that window cleaner who used to come round – huge fellow with red hair?'

'I think so – yes. Haven't seen him for ages, though. Why?'

'Well it turns out that the reason you haven't seen him is because he's in prison. He's beaten his wife up so badly that they think she'll die.'

'Fanny, how awful! Poor woman.'

'Horrible, isn't it? I always thought he looked a bit of a thug though, didn't you?'

'He certainly didn't look very nice.'

'And, Camilla, what do you think about Patrick?'

'Patrick? I don't think about him very often if I can help it. What's he done?'

'Well, I was just thinking about him. He is rather peculiar, isn't he? All that gossiping and creeping around and oiling up to people. Do you think he might be one of those people who indulge in – oh what's the damn thing called? Do-it-yourself strangulation or something?'

VIII

Walter was in love with Annie. Hopelessly, passionately in love. He thought about her all day, first thing in the morning and last thing at night, in the tube, in his office, as he dressed, as he washed, as he played the piano. Not surprisingly he was having considerable difficulty concentrating on his work, which in itself was extraordinary, since for years this work which fascinated him had provided a *raison d'être*. It gave him a sense of purpose, and was the only thing apart from music totally to absorb him and which made waking up in the morning bearable.

Walter's father, an old-fashioned disciplinarian and a taciturn man, had been headmaster of a primary school in Norfolk. His mother, with her dark Indian eyes, was a depressive whom Walter mostly remembered sitting staring vacantly into space or weeping. No one ever seemed to ask what the matter was and Walter never remembered his father addressing her except in the most perfunctory way. They must have been very unhappy and perhaps had both been relieved to follow one another to an early grave. Walter had never discovered why his mother was so dark. On the only occasion he had dared to ask, his father had told him curtly that personal questions were odious. He had often wondered where the truth lay. Since he had no memory of his maternal grandparents, anything might have been the case.

Such parents inevitably caused Walter and his older sister to withdraw into themselves, but they were clever and both took refuge in work. Walter's sister had never married and Walter suspected that she had inherited their mother's depressive nature. After Oxford she had done a Ph.D. and for years now had been teaching politics at London University. She was pale and thin and gloomy and Walter, though fond of her in a detached sort of way, only saw her from time to time; mostly if he was going away and wanted her to look in and feed Fred.

His own brief experience of marriage had left him wounded and sad and quite unprepared to attempt to repeat the exercise. All around him he saw marriages and relationships breaking up or − worse still − couples living together on sufferance. He felt that he was lucky to have a job that he liked so much, lucky in his friends and lucky, too, to be able so easily to spend time alone − to be content with his own company. But now everything had suddenly changed, leaving him quite dazed and with a strange feeling of having almost lost his identity.

Suddenly Annie, whom Walter had known slightly for several years, seemed perfect to him. She appeared to have no faults and although he had always thought of her as pretty in a dark, unaffected, almost apologetic way, he now realised that she was more beautiful than Cleopatra or Helen, wiser, gentler, kinder, sweeter and cleverer than any woman he had ever known. He felt young, light-hearted and light-headed in a way that he had never dreamed he could feel again. He was so in love with Annie in what he regarded as quite a teenage fashion, that for the time being he was content to live from moment to moment, counting the days until he saw her again, catching his breath lest she appear suddenly round the next corner, dreaming of excuses to ring her up, fantasising about her breaking off with Will, moving into his house, about eating, sleeping, living with her. But Will was, of course, the stumbling block which he hadn't yet fully confronted.

Sometimes Walter felt that this great love could never end; it had taken him over so entirely that he lived it and breathed it; it was his life-blood, his food, his drink, his hope, his belief, his everything. At other times, he allowed himself to think momentarily of Will who was due home so soon now and of the hopelessness of his passion; and then he thought that this, too, would pass. But he didn't want it to.

When he rang Annie to see whether or not she would be going to Somerset for the weekend, he was momentarily struck by a terrible fear. He felt his stomach lurch and a wave of nausea broke over him. Annie sounded so distant, almost cold, and clearly didn't want to go on talking. It took him a moment or two, after putting down the telephone, to realise that this might merely have been because she had someone with her. Why hadn't he asked her? He could so easily have done. He spent the rest of the day needlessly worrying about what Annie really felt about going away for the weekend, and looking at his watch almost every ten minutes to see how long it was before he might reasonably call her again. He only managed to get through a quarter of the work he had intended to do before the end of the day.

Walter had been really looking forward to an expedition to Mali and Niger later in the year. At the invitation of the Mali government, he and a colleague were due to go to investigate some fifty-five-million-year-old fossil turtles. He had always longed for an opportunity to visit the Niger valley and to see where the great seaways once crossed the Sahara. But suddenly fossil turtles and prehistoric seaways had lost their allure, unless Annie could visit them with him which was, of course, out of the question. Nevertheless Walter expended a great deal of energy wildly imagining circumstances which might bring Annie to Mali just when he was there.

As for Annie, she was feeling slightly embarrassed by how curt she had been to Walter on the telephone. It annoyed her to think that she must have sounded quite unfriendly. She would ring him as soon as he returned from work to explain. He knew exactly how tricky Sarah could be, and it was certainly Sarah's presence alone which had prevented her from saying quite how much she was looking forward to the weekend.

In fact Annie was looking forward to the weekend more than she had looked forward to anything for months. Walter was easy company, humorous, tactful and interesting to talk to. His was a world about which she knew nothing and which formerly she would never have imagined being attracted to, but which had now begun to fascinate her. Where once she would have said 'boring old fossils', she found herself, like a curious child, asking the most elementary and, she supposed, idiotic questions about brachiopoda and the Lower Cretaceous period – things she had never even heard of before. It was refreshing to meet new people and she felt flattered that Walter's friends had liked her enough to invite her for the weekend. The cottage they had was near a place called Kilve on the Bristol Channel. Walter was delighted by the fact that the coast there was the only place in Western Europe where you could look through a continuous sequence of terrestrial deposits from the Triassic period to marine deposits of the Jurassic period. This was all beyond Annie and she laughed at Walter for liking nothing that was less than fifty million years old. But she remembered how she had hated geography lessons at school and how tedious and pointless it had seemed then, to be drawing and labelling layers of sandstone and limestone and God knows what. Now she wished she had paid a little more attention. Layers of sandstone suddenly seemed quite interesting, even if she had no idea when the Triassic or Jurassic periods were.

They left London on Saturday morning in Walter's car and as they stopped to turn into the Bayswater Road, Isabel crossed the street in front of them, carrying a huge shopping basket. She waved to Walter and mouthed a 'hallo', then, as she spotted Annie in the passenger seat, she did a double take and waved again.

Annie longed to tell Walter that Sarah and Fanny and Camilla and people were putting it around that he was having an affair with Isabel, but she decided against it. It was a dangerous topic of conversation which might encourage quite what reaction Annie didn't know. She sensed that Walter was growing fond of her, but she presumed that he intended to keep the relationship on a platonic level, although you could never be sure. In any case she certainly had no desire to intimate that it might be otherwise. Before the gossip about Isabel, Sarah, of course, had been saying that Walter was gay. Annie instinctively felt that he wasn't. But you could never be sure about that either. Annie wished Sarah didn't talk so much. She didn't want her head filled with theories which could only serve to blur her own perception. If Walter was gay, let him be gay, she thought, and if he was having an affair with Isabel, let him get on with it. It was no business of hers and yet a gut reaction informed her that she wanted neither of these things to be true.

She glanced at Walter sitting beside her. He looked relaxed and self-contained in a rather intriguing way. Little did she imagine quite how tense and excited he felt, how joyful to have her sitting there with him, how happy to think that he would have her company for the next two days. He longed to put out a hand and touch her, but knew that he must not.

The weather was fine and the roads clear so they made good time almost to Walter's disappointment, as he knew that as soon as they arrived, he would no longer have Annie to himself.

Annie felt that she was going away on a real holiday. She had never been to Somerset before and it almost seemed to her like abroad. She had given her telephone number to Tamsin in case of emergency, but hardly expected her to get in touch, so for once she felt carefree, properly away from home and away from her everyday worries about which her hosts, thank God, knew nothing.

The weather was fine and the sea was grey and as they walked along the coast after lunch, Walter mumbled something about terrestrial deposits and the Jurassic period and Annie didn't mind what he was talking about because she was happy and the gentle, red-brown Somerset hills curved softly down to pastureland and the sea.

The fossil elephant man and his wife were good cooks and hospitable hosts; their cottage was small but comfortable with a big, shaggy garden and a view across farmland to the sea. From behind the cottage you could walk straight up through steep, watery, wooded valleys to the top of the Quantock Hills. Under these same oak trees and by these same babbling brooks, Wordsworth, Coleridge and Dorothy Wordsworth had once all been wont to walk, which, Annie had to admit, she found far more exciting than all the layers of sandstone in Europe.

Annie was grateful to Walter for the tact with which he made it clear that he and she had not come as a couple but that she had been separately invited in her own right, so by the time they left on Sunday after a long walk and an excellent lunch, Annie felt that she had really made new friends of her own.

Fossil elephant, whose name was Cedric, felt about the Quantocks very much as many people feel about their local beauty spot, that he owned them in some way, and so he was especially gratified when Annie gasped in awe at the sight of a huge stag which appeared as from nowhere, just up the side of the hill from where they were walking. It stopped and turned its great head to look down on them coolly from above before deciding that they presented no threat to its autonomy and moving off gracefully, to disappear into the woods from whence it came.

When they reached the top of the hill, Annie gasped again at the quite unexpected splendour of what she saw. The hills appeared to be surrounded by sea.

'That's North Hill and Minehead over there, and Exmoor.' Cedric, in his woolly jersey, pointed proprietorially in one direction. He wore real walking boots, laced above the ankles. 'And Wales is over there.' He stretched out his other arm.

Annie looked out across moorland, over the woods huddling down in the combe beneath her to where two little islands hovered between the grey of the sky and the grey of the sea, apparently uncertain as to where they belonged. Even in winter, even on a dull day with the Welsh coast invisible, it was an enchanted land. London seemed far away and dirty and sad and irrelevant.

Cedric and Sandy were not returning to London until the middle of the week, but both Annie and Walter felt a wrench as they waved goodbye and set off back to the city. As they sped back up the M4 and London loomed nearer, so did Annie's problems seem to begin once again to enclose her, to take possession of her. She had promised Tamsin she would be home for supper and besides she had some classes to prepare before morning. Back she raced towards Tamsin and Henry and people who didn't really want to learn English, and to Will.

But Walter was speeding back to what had suddenly, after all these years, become the loneliness of his own arid, passionless little house. He wished he could share it not with an inscrutable iguana, but with Annie who would give it life. When could he reasonably hope even to see her again? The journey for them both passed exceptionally quickly.

As they drew up outside Annie's house, Patrick happened to be in his sitting-room, vaguely looking out of the window. He noticed the car stop under a street lamp and he saw Annie and Walter get out; he watched as Walter went round to the boot, opened it and took out Annie's suitcase. He watched him carry it up the steps to her front door; he watched as Annie and Walter kissed each other on both cheeks and as Annie inserted her key in the lock and turned to wave to Walter who ran down the steps and got back into his car.

Annie, as she waved once more, noticed the net curtain in Patrick's house being tweaked back into place. An outward and visible sign of the claustrophobic atmosphere which she was beginning to feel whenever she returned to her house. But this time it seemed to weigh more heavily than ever. She thought as she pushed open her front door that she didn't want the whole neighbourhood talking about her weekend and wondering where she had been and what was going on between her and Walter. Nothing was going on between her and Walter. But she wished he had come in with her. Tamsin didn't appear to be back and the house felt hollow. Perhaps she would just ring Walter in a few minutes, to thank him for the lift. But then she wondered what on earth he would think of her. She had thanked him quite adequately just now. There was no need to say any more.

Some junk mail lay dead on the mat inside the front door proclaiming the emptiness of the house. Annie kicked it impatiently to one side and went on upstairs with her suitcase.

Just as she reached her bedroom, the telephone rang with sudden shrill insistency. She nearly jumped out of her skin. It was Will.

'I've been trying to get hold of you all weekend,' he said, somewhat irritably.

Walter had been quite elated by the weekend, but as he left Annie on her doorstep, he suddenly felt bereft of everything. She had asked him in for a drink, but he had refused, thinking that Tamsin would probably prefer to have her mother to herself.

He was glad that Annie had got on so well with his friends, but what he did not realise was that Cedric's and Sandy's invitation had not been entirely devoid of guile. For years now they had longed to find someone for Walter who, to them, seemed sad and lonely, a disappointed man. They had taken an instant liking to Annie when they met having a drink at Walter's house, and suspecting him of being too lazy, or too hesitant to go for it, they decided to give a little encouragement and invite them together for the weekend. Will they did not take into account. That evening they congratulated themselves on a job well done.

'He's a fool if he lets her slip through his fingers,' said Cedric. He was putting dubbin on his walking boots.

'I hope he doesn't,' said Sandy as she poured herself a glass of wine. 'But apparently she's got some sort of a man. She said something about his being in Bosnia.'

'Too bad,' said Cedric, as he placed the boots neatly

side by side on the draining board and looked admiringly at them.

Little did they imagine Walter, pacing at that moment restlessly around his little house, quite unable to relax, quite unable to think of anything but Annie, wondering what possible excuse he could have for ringing her at once, only ten minutes after having left her. He thought that while he dialled the number some inspiration as to a reason for his call might come to him out of the blue. He did so and was partly relieved to find it engaged. He looked at his watch and decided it was supper time, but he wasn't hungry. Perhaps he would have a drink, but nothing tempted him. He began to play the piano but stopped again almost immediately. Walter had not felt like this for a very long time. The weekend had only made matters worse.

Of course the gossips had not been idle during those last two days. In fact they had been thrown into some kind of disarray by Isabel's report of having seen Walter and Annie setting out together on Saturday morning. No one appeared to have any idea as to where they might have been going. Guesses as to their destination varied widely from Sainsbury's, Paris and Brighton to the Battersea Dogs Home. Sarah was perfectly furious and spent a large part of the weekend telephoning both Annie and Walter to check that they really were away. The longer they appeared to be gone, the angrier she became. On Sunday evening, Patrick had the great satisfaction of being able to ring Fanny to tell her what he had just witnessed.

Father Leatham tended to agree with Henry about sending Tamsin to a convent for her 'A' levels. He was entirely of the opinion that most, if not all, the child's problems stemmed from the fact of having a working mother. He was also a little in love with Angie and so took the opportunity to bring the conversation round to her and to what a perfect Christian mother she was, conforming to the Pauline ideal of womanhood – he'd conveniently forgotten about the pill – submitting to her husband in everything just as the Church submits to Christ. He gave a coy little laugh which made Henry feel momentarily uneasy.

'The feminists have done untold harm', the priest went on, 'by forgetting that woman is God's gift to man, that she was fashioned from the rib of Adam. You have only to refer to St Paul's epistle to the Corinthians – you know it well, of course.'

Even Henry's faith had not prevented the fog around his mind from being permeated by the knowledge that the story of Adam and Eve was generally believed to be mythical, even in the highest theological circles. Neither did he want to dwell on the subject of Angie's submission, but he was comforted to find support for his plans for his daughter. Perhaps it was a good thing after all that Tamsin was coming for the weekend; he would be able to talk to her about her schooling and tell her directly what he intended instead of having to deal with the matter through Annie who seemed to have an annoying habit of almost intentionally refusing to understand what he was saying.

This time, when he collected Tamsin from the station, he was relieved to find her apparently in a more amenable and communicative mood. She chatted pleasantly about this and that and school and her exams without referring to whatever it was that she had particularly wanted to talk to him about. His anxieties were for the time being lulled and he even felt quite optimistic that Tamsin might agree without any fuss to his suggestion. Only he wasn't quite sure when or how to broach it.

Tamsin, on the other hand, was in such a confused state

that she had quite forgotten exactly what it was she had wanted to say to her father when she invited herself for the weekend. All she could remember was the disgust with which she had reacted to the revolting suggestion put to her by India and to the awareness that that was what the gossips – some of whom masqueraded as her mother's friends – were saying about her. For some reason the great build-up of resentment and anger she had felt about her father seemed to be brushed aside at a single stroke, to be replaced by fierce loyalty and violent indignation against anyone who dared to accuse Henry of anything so vile. To accuse her either, for that matter, since it seemed to her that to accuse one was to accuse the other. For these reasons Tamsin had felt an upsurge of solidarity with Henry, but she had never, at any minute, considered repeating to him what she had heard.

In this moment of solidarity she suddenly felt that she could forgive her father anything. She could forgive him for leaving her mother, for the lies and the silly annulment; she could even forgive him for marrying that awful Angie – she wasn't too bad really, Tamsin supposed. The horrid baby still presented a bit of a stumbling block, but then, even he hadn't asked to be born. Tamsin could forgive Henry all these things because he was innocent of that most repulsive of all crimes and because people were telling lies about him. About her father.

Such was Tamsin's mood of conciliation that she managed to behave quite well throughout Saturday, despite being reconfirmed in her original opinion that Angie was a bitch, and even thought that she might go to mass on Sunday, just to show everyone.

Henry, of course, was delighted and wanted only the courage to find the right moment for a discussion with his daughter about her education, but Angie scoffed and assured Henry that Tamsin must just want to get something out of him. Angie was not prepared to be softened up by her stepdaughter and was perfectly convinced that Henry was up against more than he was bargaining for if he thought he could easily persuade her to go to boarding-school.

'For one thing,' she said, as she lay propped against her pillows that night, vaguely looking for her place in the latest Jilly Cooper, 'she may have a boyfriend she doesn't want to leave.'

'A boyfriend!' Henry was carefully tying his pyjama cord in a neat bow. 'Of course she hasn't got a boyfriend. We'd know if she had.'

Angie gave a disdainful 'pfoof' and turned her attention to her book.

As Henry climbed into bed, he glanced at his wife. She was very pretty, but he suddenly felt that he and she lived in different worlds and that ultimately there could be no coming together. He wondered what made her say that about Tamsin. Did she know something he didn't know, or was she just trying to provoke him, or did she get such ideas from the silly literature she read? Sometimes he wished she would read something a little more serious than Jilly Cooper and the *Daily Mail*.

Jilly Cooper on this occasion didn't hold Angie's attention for long as she soon turned out the light and fell asleep, but Henry couldn't sleep and could only think of what Angie had said about Tamsin and a boyfriend.

It could hardly be true – Tamsin wasn't yet sixteen. Henry was presuming the implication was that sex was involved, about which, in relation to his daughter, he recoiled from thinking. It was most unpleasing. Surely Annie would not encourage that. Young people, he knew, were up to anything and everything these days at a terrifyingly early age. But surely not Tamsin at fifteen.

Henry himself, having been very tense and awkward as

a young man and coming, as he did, from a strait-laced Catholic family, had been far from the vanguard of the so-called free and easy generation in which he had grown up. He expected his daughter in so many ways to be like him. If she had a boyfriend, why didn't he know about it? Was Annie keeping something from him on purpose? The more he thought about it, the more his thoughts went round and round in circles and the more he wished he could think of anything else at all. But when he tried, he could only think of Lloyd's and where he was going to get the money from to send Tamsin away to school; so then he thought about Tamsin again and about her boyfriend and about her and sex and then he felt queasy and almost wished he didn't have a daughter and that sex had never been invented. Eventually, in despair, he got up and went downstairs and paced around the house feeling trapped, trying to compose a disapproving letter to Annie in his head. After all, it was all Annie's fault. She clearly had no idea how to bring up a daughter properly, how to give her any proper sense of Christian morality. That wasn't supposed to be his job.

In the morning Henry was feeling pretty rough from his lack of sleep, but he was encouraged to forget his anxieties of the night before by Tamsin saying that she would come to church.

Henry felt proud as he walked into the horrid little modern church which, he sometimes thought, looked more like a health centre than a church, with Tamsin at his side. He walked tall and nodded graciously to all the people he knew as he strode down the aisle, searching for two empty seats in the already crowded nave. People came from miles around to hear Father Leatham's sermons and above all to confess to him. He had a truly old-fashioned way of finding a means of letting you off the hook if you happened to be someone he knew and of whom he approved.

Angie had stayed at home because she had a headache. In fact she didn't have a headache at all but was lying in bed, deeply immersed in her Jilly Cooper and glad to have the house to herself for the moment. The baby was in his cot, snoozing.

It was on the way home that Henry decided to approach his daughter about her future – and for that matter about her present. And it was on the way home that Tamsin finally cracked. She could not behave well any longer – church and Father Leatham and all that genuflecting and offering of the sign of peace and taking of communion was too much for her. In fact she very rarely thought about religion, associating it entirely with grown-ups and bossiness and eating what is put in front of you and not watching too much television and reading 'good' books and having no freedom, but when she was forced to, she would glibly announce that it was all rubbish. It never occurred to her that cleverer, more reflective people than she had been thinking about Christianity for two thousand years without quite daring to dismiss it, and that therefore it was worth at least pausing for.

She had meant this morning to go quietly with her father to mass, to think of something else while it was going on and to come away with the satisfaction of having shown some solidarity with Henry. But when Henry started to talk to her in what she regarded as a patronising way about how pleased he was to see her in church and about how glad he was to realise that she had not lost her faith, she couldn't take it.

'I couldn't give a toss about God or the Pope,' she suddenly screamed. 'I don't believe in any of it. I only came because of you and because of what people are saying about you – nothing to do with bloody God!' And she burst into tears.

At the first sign of emotion from any quarter, Henry's instinct was to dive for cover – to get out of the room, to leave the house, to turn on the television, to hide behind the paper, to change the subject – to escape. But there was nothing much he could do at the moment, stuck in the car with Tamsin, heading for home. He felt utterly miserable.

In Henry's eyes the emotions were there quite simply to be controlled – controlled by reason. Henry, of course, regarded himself as an eminently reasonable man and his reason had led him to the conclusion that women were very rarely, if ever, as reasonable as men. It never occurred to him to think that two equally reasonable beings, starting from different premisses, were bound to reach different conclusions, nor did it occur to him that a premiss from which he started might be faulty. In all the disagreements he had ever had with either of his wives, his daughter or his mother, he had never been able to see the other person's point of view. All he could see was a woman, tossing her head, careering around, blindly illogical as a loose horse. To confirm these prejudices he clung to the blinkered male's last bastion of hope: that women are rarely very good at chess.

A couple of years before, Tamsin, aged only thirteen, had tossed her head and asked him if he'd ever heard of testosterone. 'Chess is a very aggressive game,' she'd said. 'You need testosterone to give you the desire to win.'

Henry had been embarrassed to hear his daughter using words like testosterone, and slightly shocked that she even knew what it was. He'd just laughed in a dismissive way and changed the subject.

Now he felt that to laugh like that would be quite inappropriate. Once again he thought of a loose horse – wildly out of control. He didn't think to ask Tamsin what she meant, why she was crying, or to allow her to explain what she saw as the problem. Nor did he deign to enquire what it was they were saying about him. He felt threatened and if he couldn't escape, then attack must be the best form of defence.

'Do stop crying,' he said irritably. 'And grow up and stop talking such nonsense. You are guilty of the sin of pride and if you can't behave properly, I suggest that you stay away until you can. There is no point in coming down here just to upset everybody.' Suddenly Henry had got the bit between his teeth and he went on to say everything he had wanted to say to his daughter for a long time now. He told her that she was rude and unfriendly to Angie, that her attitude to the baby, Matthew, was horrid. He told her that she had no manners, that she was selfish and spoilt and lazy, that he had no idea what she got up to in London and that he didn't like to think that she might be misbehaving with boys, that she had no sense of responsibility and that the best thing for her would be to spend the next two years in a convent school where she might learn to do some work, but where she might also learn some manners and to have a proper respect for her faith. He added insult to injury by remarking just as they reached the house, 'I really don't understand your mother.'

Almost before the car had stopped Tamsin jumped angrily out and slammed the door. With tears streaming down her face, but without saying anything, she ran upstairs to her room to collect her things. When she came down a few moments later, having wiped her eyes, she looked coldly at her father and said haughtily, 'If you don't want to take me to the station, I'll call a taxi.'

Henry drove her to the station in silence.

'Hallo.'

135

'Hallo, Fanny!'

'Camilla, hi!'

'Did Annie ring you last night?'

'No, why?'

'Apparently she'd lost Tamsin. She rang Isabel because she thought Tamsin might have gone round here. The two girls are quite friendly.'

'I don't think they are, you know. I'd say Tamsin was much closer to my India. But it's hardly surprising if Tamsin wasn't at home last night. After all, Annie was away all weekend – with Walter.'

'I know, I heard about that. What about Isabel?'

'I can't make out what's going on; but I would have thought that Annie ought to be around for her daughter at a time like this.'

'I couldn't agree more. But what do you think can have happened between Walter and Isabel?'

'I can't imagine. What do you think happened?'

'Well I think something very odd's going on. You see, there's no doubt about it, but Walter must be a bit peculiar. Some people think he's gay, don't they? Well, perhaps he isn't. But I still think there's something – well – just a bit strange – those black eyes. Perhaps he's into something kinky and Isabel didn't like it.'

'Yes. That's probably right. Anyway Isabel's bound to find someone else quite easily.'

'Oh, Isabel – she'll be all right.'

'I'm sure she will.'

'Maybe she has found somebody else.'

'Perhaps she has. But where do you think Tamsin's got to?'

'I should have thought that if she wasn't at home, she'd have gone to her boyfriend.'

'Yes, but Annie wouldn't have found her there

because, according to India, Annie doesn't know anything about him.'

'I can't understand Annie. But do you know what I think? I think that Isabel has somehow off-loaded Walter onto Annie. Just a way of getting rid of him.'

'I wouldn't be surprised. But what's going to happen when Will gets back?'

'God knows.'

'Hallo Fanny? It's Sarah.'

'How're you then?'

'I'm absolutely furious.'

'Why? What's happened?'

'It's Annie. Wouldn't you be furious if you had to hear all about your best friend through some ridiculous, gossiping grapevine? First of all Isabel tells me that Walter and Annie have gone off somewhere for a dirty weekend and then, last night, you rang to tell me that Patrick had seen them coming back. Fancy having to hear something like that from Patrick of all people! I mean, it's too awful. And why on earth did Camilla put it about in the first place that Walter was having an affair with Isabel? We all thought that was true, didn't we?'

'I can't remember who knew about that first. Anyway, I think it was true. Camilla says it was true and that there was something not very nice about Walter – she didn't say what – but something a bit funny – you know – and so Isabel off-loaded him onto Annie. It sounds very likely. Isabel's quite crafty and very tough and Annie – well I suppose Annie's a bit lonely what with Will never being there. She probably decided to have a quick fling. Will's coming back next week I think.'

'Annie's never understood Will. That's one thing I've always known and I should be right about that. After all, Will is one of my oldest friends . . .'

IX

'I say, Camilla . . .'

'Fanny! What's the news?'

'I've just had Sarah on the telephone. She's furious.'

'Why? What about?'

'She's furious with Annie – and Walter – and Patrick – and Isabel. Anyone you can think of, in fact.'

'How ridiculous. It's all because she's jealous, you know. I've always said so. She's jealous of Annie in a way, and she's jealous of Walter. I don't suppose there's much for her to be jealous of Patrick about, though.'

'She hates him knowing something before she does, that's all.'

'Well, she's just jealous. You've said so yourself, I know. But I'll tell you something. There's going to be a terrific hoo-ha when Will gets back. And no doubt Patrick will have his net curtains twitching at all hours, so he'll be able to keep us informed.'

'But do you really believe everything Patrick says?'

'Well, even if it's not true, it's quite fun.'

'I say, Camilla, do you think Patrick talks about us the same way he talks about everyone else? I've never thought of that before.'

'Of course he does – if he can find anything to say. I can't think what he could possibly find to say about me, though.'

'Or me, for that matter.'

'Don't worry, if he doesn't know anything, he'll just invent something, don't you think?'

'What cheek! I'd be furious if he invented something about me. I mean, people might believe it.'

'Oh, don't worry about that, no one ever believes gossip. They just hear it and then forget it immediately.'

'I suppose so.'

'By the way, did you know that Walter's wife divorced him for mental cruelty?'

'Gosh! Really? How awful! Who told you?'

'Well, it's just something I happen to know. I don't think it's entirely surprising, do you? But can you imagine wanting to have anything to do with someone like that?'

'No. It would be too awful. Do you suppose that that's why Isabel gave him the push?'

'I'm sure it is.'

'Did you ever know Walter's wife?'

'No. But apparently she was incredibly sweet. She had a terrible time with him.'

'How dreadful! But why didn't you ever tell me before?'

'Well, it's not really the sort of thing one passes on.'

'No. I suppose not. What do you think he's done for sex ever since?'

'Dinosaurs?'

'Oh, Camilla, you are awful! But what about Annie? Why on earth do you think she's suddenly gone off with him?'

'I can't imagine. Perhaps she likes kinky people. I mean, look at Henry – you know – him and Tamsin.'

'Some people are peculiar.'

'I say, Fanny, I must go now, but if you hear anything about Tamsin – do let me know. After all, one can't help feeling a bit concerned for the poor girl and wondering what she's up to – how she's getting on. If I were Annie, I'd kill Henry . . .'

Neil was at home and driving Sarah mad. When he was away she moaned about the amount of time she was obliged to spend alone, but now that he had been around for a little while, she was longing for him to go away again. She was fed up with shopping for him and with providing a proper meal every evening. Besides that, he got on her nerves. He never seemed to listen to anything she had to say and when he did, he never seemed to understand her point of view. She was appalled by his attitude to the rumours about Tamsin and Henry.

'I should think it's most unlikely to be true,' he said at breakfast, disappearing back behind the *Independent*.

'You can't just dismiss it like that because you don't want it to be true,' Sarah replied crossly. Then she went on and on and on about India and Fanny and what Tamsin had and had not said to India and what Isabel had said to Fanny and Fanny had said to Camilla. She went on about Annie and Henry and Will and Walter. Occasionally Neil gave a grunt from behind the newspaper, which generally provoked a new stream of angry monologue.

'You don't understand anything,' she said desperately.

Neil stood up and folded the paper. 'I wouldn't worry about it so much, if I were you. It's only gossip.'

'Gossip!' Sarah almost screamed. 'How can you say it's gossip? For one thing, I don't gossip. It's not gossip when you are genuinely concerned about other people – and all these people are my friends. Don't you realise that I'm worried about them. Your trouble is that you only think of your work – and money and the next bloody conference you're going to. I'm concerned with human beings.'

Neil sighed. He didn't know what to say or how to defend himself. 'I'm afraid I'd better be thinking about my work now,' he said apologetically, looking at his watch, 'or I'll be late. I've got a rather important meeting with some Japanese . . .'

'Then there's Annie getting involved with Walter who, as it turns out, is some kind of sado-masochist which is why Isabel gave him the push.' Sarah spoke to her husband's retreating back.

Neil sudddenly swung round. 'What are you talking about? You cannot go around saying things like that about people,' he said.

'Why should that suddenly worry you so much?'

'Well I thought you said that all those people were your friends. I don't think they'd be very pleased to hear you.'

'I'm only talking to my own husband in the privacy of my own house, so please don't accuse me of "going around" and telling everybody. But it's certainly a matter for concern. I'm concerned about Annie – and Will for that matter – and Walter. He needs to see a psycho-sexual doodah – psychotherapist, psychologist, whatever they're called – if you ask me.'

Neil couldn't stand any more of it. He longed for his business meeting and for the quietly spoken courteous Japanese who would not be screaming at him about psycho-sexual doodahs. 'See you this evening,' he said. 'I must dash.' And he bolted for the door.

Sarah cleared up the breakfast things savagely, almost throwing the cups and saucers into the washing-up machine. How dared Neil treat her like that, in such a patronising way, and how dared he sit there so smugly behind the newspaper – he would take the bloody *Independent* – talking about Japanese businessmen? How dared he mind about some Japanese businessmen he'd probably never see again more than he minded about her friends? Come to that, they were supposed to be his friends too. Except that a cold fish like him didn't have real friends, of course. That was the trouble. Neil was a cold fish. Why had she never realised it before? And how could someone like her – so warm and vital – be expected to get on with a cold fish like Neil? It didn't seem fair.

As she swept the butter dish impatiently off the table, it slipped from Sarah's grasp, fell to the floor and broke into several pieces. She swore as she bent down to pick them up. Everything was going wrong for Sarah and everyone was upsetting her. She thought she ought to try to talk to Annie again, but she was irritated by the thought of her old friend and what she regarded as Annie's two-faced behaviour. Perhaps she would speak to Walter. But the thought of him was even more painful. Sarah felt let down, ignored, unwanted, ill-used – all of which manifested itself in righteous indignation at what she saw as Walter's treachery. She was not accustomed to analysing her feelings too carefully nor did she generally ask herself too many questions.

In the end she decided that Isabel was the person to approach. She hadn't worked out why she wanted to see Isabel, or what it was that she might have to say to her. She merely sensed that she wanted to see her – just to look at her really, to sum her up. There was a lot about Isabel which she felt she hadn't taken in and suddenly she was interested in her. She would ring Isabel and ask her to lunch. If Isabel was upset about Walter, she might even confide in Sarah and then Sarah, as Walter's old and close friend, might find it incumbent upon her to have a word with him. She wouldn't be afraid to tell him that he needed help. Annie had had quite a hard time, the last thing she needed now was to become involved with a sado-masochist. Then there was Will. When he came home, he'd be wanting to cry on Sarah's shoulder. Sarah's friends always turned to her in distress.

Sarah found Isabel strangely evasive on the telephone. She couldn't come to lunch any day that week and didn't even seem to want to chat very much. But Sarah was not going to let her off the hook too easily.

'What do you think about Walter and Annie?' she asked bluntly.

'I don't know. What do you mean?' Isabel sounded hesitant.

'I thought you were the one who saw them on Saturday, setting out together. I mean, I'm delighted for them both, if that's what they want. Of course I've known the pair of them for years – years.' Sarah at her most sincere.

'Well, I don't know anything about them.' Isabel was distant. 'It's up to them where they go. Listen, Sarah, I'm sorry – I have to go out. I can't talk now.'

'But you've been so close to Walter, I thought you might be concerned about him.'

Isabel ignored the impertinent innuendo and just said, 'Look, I'm sorry about lunch – another time – but thanks all the same. I must go now. 'Bye.'

Sarah remembered the time Isabel had come to supper and left so early and decided that Isabel had problems. She wasn't a very friendly person really. It was quite surprising Walter had ever bothered to have anything to do with her. Perhaps it was *faute de mieux*. It suddenly occurred to Sarah that in fact he had probably had a weakness for her, Sarah, all along. Why had she never realised – not that she had ever found him particularly attractive. She would never have bothered with him in that way. So naturally he had turned to Isabel. Sarah liked the idea of Isabel as second best.

143

She was still in her dressing-gown, an expensive pink-and-white tailored affair which, she thought crossly as she glanced at the satin cuffs, needed to go to the cleaners. She was fiddling round in the kitchen wondering how to spend the rest of the day, picking things up absent-mindedly and putting them down again without rhyme or reason, when the telephone rang.

It was Annie. Sarah didn't feel like seeing Annie – or even talking to her. But Annie sounded serious and even worried. She had problems with Tamsin which Sarah would understand she didn't want to discuss, but Annie was turning to Sarah as a friend, not that she supposed Sarah could do very much to help in this instance. It was just that Annie knew there was a lot of gossip around – Sarah was bound to have heard it. Please could she just deny it or stamp on it whenever she got an opportunity. None of it could do anyone any good.

Sarah was all over Annie. 'Of course,' she said earnestly. 'I'll do anything I can – but I mean, what's it all about?'

'Oh, Sarah, you know perfectly well what it's about. Just tell everybody it's not true.'

'I do hope it isn't – not that I would ever believe something like that.' Sarah sounded very caring.

'Of course it's not true.' Annie sounded angry. 'I can't really imagine that anyone could have believed it for an instant, but, unfortunately, poeple who gossip want such things to be true.'

'Don't be silly, of course they don't. No one would want to believe a thing like that about someone they knew.'

'Do you know what?' Annie was unusually belligerent. 'Since I've been living here, I've come to the conclusion that people's lives are shaped by gossip.'

'Oh, come on – isn't that going a bit too far?'

'Well, I'll tell you about it one day, but it's certainly

true that people often do things they wouldn't do if the idea hadn't been put into their head by other people's idle talk.'

'I find that hard to believe,' said Sarah.

'Well, I can assure you it's true.'

'And, by the way, just to change the subject, Annie, have you seen Walter lately?' Sarah thought she was being quite crafty.

'Yes. I saw him at the weekend.' And Annie felt like adding, 'which you know perfectly well.' Instead she said nothing.

'Do you think he's still seeing Isabel?' was what Sarah wanted to know next.

'Why don't you ask him – or Isabel?' Annie enquired.

'Oh, I don't know. Maybe I've just become a dull person, but Walter doesn't seem to want to see me these days. I don't know what I've done wrong. We used to see each other every day.'

In fact there had never been a time when Walter and Sarah saw each other every day, but Annie who was a naturally straightforward person accepted the information quite happily. It didn't bother her. In any case, she had far more important things on her mind. She wished, as she put the telephone down, that Sarah wasn't so tricky. What had become of her old friend? One problem was that Sarah listened to too much gossip and everything she heard made her jealous, angry, resentful or sorry for herself. Poor Sarah.

But Annie was too concerned about Tamsin to be able to spend very much time worrying about Sarah and her problems. She had waited till after half-past eight on Sunday evening before telephoning Henry to find out what train Tamsin caught home and had been appalled to discover that she had left, in what Henry described as an 'emotional condition', before lunch. Annie spent the rest of the evening in a fevered state ringing anywhere where she thought Tamsin might be, ringing Henry, the hospitals and the police. She hadn't gone to bed all night, let alone slept, so that in the morning she had had to ring in to say that she was in no fit state to go to work.

Annie did not discover Tamsin's whereabouts and the fact that she was safe, even if all hell was about to break loose, until late on Monday morning, by which time her anxiety had hardly been allayed by a series of most unpleasant telephone calls from various men making unimaginably obscene suggestions. She couldn't make head or tail of what was going on but it made her feel very uneasy. At first she just thought it was a case of a wrong number but after two or three calls of the same nature, she began to suspect something more sinister although she couldn't begin to imagine what. The whole world suddenly seemed to be topsy turvy.

Thank God, she thought, for Walter. She had needed a friend last night and had finally succumbed to the temptation to ring Walter to tell him her troubles. He had come round immediately and stayed until she eventually insisted he go. He had been a source of enormous support and had rung again first thing in the morning to see if she had any news. Now, amidst all the turmoil of her concern for Tamsin, another feeling was beginning to intrude. She was beginning to miss Walter, to long for the end of the day when she might see him again. She asked herself if she was falling in love and decided that she wasn't. Walter was just a very good friend and she needed a friend at a time like this – with Will away. She couldn't afford to fall in love at the moment. Life was complicated enough already.

What Patrick had missed, despite having his nose almost permanently glued to his window pane, was the sight of Walter coming round on foot to Annie's house at about ten o'clock that evening, sprinting lightly up the front doorsteps and ringing the bell. He remained there till the early hours when Annie insisted that he go home to get some sleep. Patrick who, due to a little trouble with his prostate, slept fitfully in the small hours between visits to the lavatory, at some moment heard a front door banging shut in the street. He instantly leapt out of bed, but by the time he reached the window, Walter, who moved swiftly and quietly, had already disappeared without trace round the corner. Patrick stared at the row of blankly closed doors on the other side of the street, tantalised by his inability to detect which of them had so recently opened to let someone in, or out into the night. He turned disappointedly away and went for another pee.

When Tamsin left Pewsey station she had no particular idea as to what she was going to do next. All she could think about at the time was getting away from Henry. As soon as she was sitting safely in the train, she wanted to cry again. She felt everything and everybody against her. She had already decided that one of the first things she must do was to get out of the sex chat line. She had still not been paid but she had begun to think that she never would be, and that the only thing to do was to cut her losses. The longer she answered that awful chat line, the more miserable it made her; it was just that for some reason she lacked the courage to deal with the situation.

Tamsin had also decided that the time had come to make a break with Billy. She had acknowledged to herself that she was afraid of him and the recognition of that fact had suddenly made her hate him. In fact she suddenly hated him so much that the idea of seeing him made her feel nauseous and the very thought of his hand on her body made her cringe with disgust. Now of course, she wondered how she could ever have liked him and even told herself that she hadn't. She felt, as she sat in the train, that she could see him for what he really was – a lazy con man with an out-of-date pony-tail who was trying to be big. She was furious with herself for ever having had anything to do with him and even more furious with herself for still being afraid of him. Afraid to tell him that she didn't ever want to see him again – that she'd never liked him in the first place.

She thought it was all her parents' fault for not having provided her with a proper home. She was sure that if she had had a proper home – whatever that might be, the house in Islington perhaps – she would never have wanted to have anything to do with someone like Billy.

Then there was the whole monstrous problem of school and the lies she told, and the builder's receipt. She was at a complete loss as to how to get out of all that.

By the time the train reached Paddington, Tamsin had ceased to feel tearful. She felt panicky instead and was still totally undecided about what she should do next. Her mother had gone away for the weekend and certainly wouldn't be home yet. Tamsin didn't want to go back to an empty house, neither did she feel like ringing any of her friends. None of them would understand.

It was just on the spur of the moment that she decided to take the tube to Shepherd's Bush. As she walked purposefully down the Goldhawk Road she became more and more convinced that what she was about to do was the only possible solution to the problem of school. When she had dealt with that, she felt she would be strong enough to sort out Billy and the chat line. She felt a sudden surge of optimism as she turned right up a small side-street. She thought she knew exactly where to find the street she was looking for, but in fact she spent some time turning down various wrong ones and retracing her tracks, during which time her determination, far from failing her, only increased and her optimism mounted.

When the front doorbell rang, Jan McLaughlin was in bed with her lover who was not only the father of one of her pupils, but another woman's husband. She nearly jumped out of her skin. Her lover jumped out of bed and hastily began pulling on his trousers.

'Don't bother,' Jan said. 'Come back into bed. I won't answer it and whoever it is will go away in a minute.' Jan certainly wasn't expecting anybody and in fact couldn't think for the life of her who might be ringing her doorbell at three o'clock on a Sunday afternoon.

Bob, her guilty lover, immediately had terrifying visions of a furious wife who, having miraculously traced him to his *nid d'amour*, stood on the doorstep with chin set, determinedly ringing the bell. She was supposed to have taken the children to her mother's for the weekend, leaving him alone in London to catch up with some work. He zipped up his trousers, stepped gingerly towards the window and tried to peer down into the street, but he dared not show himself and so was unable to see who was at the door.

Tamsin waited a moment and then pressed the bell again, long and hard. She stepped back onto the pavement and looked up at the front of the house, the top two floors of which were occupied by Miss McLaughlin and, as she did so, she thought she saw a shadow move across the window. Someone, she felt sure, was in.

'Who the hell do you think it can be?' Bob was busy tying the laces of his trainers.

'Oh, come on. Get back into bed. No one knows you're here and I'm certainly not expecting anyone.' Jan was infuriated at having her pleasures interrupted. 'It's probably the Seventh Day Adventists,' she said. 'They'll go away in a minute.' The doorbell went on ringing persistently and Bob, perched on the corner of the crumpled bed, went on tying his laces.

'How am I supposed to get out of here?' he suddenly said, panic-stricken.

Jan laughed.

'Oh do stop laughing and get dressed.' Bob was feeling edgy.

Reluctantly Jan climbed out of bed and pulled on a pair of jeans and a jersey. She ran her fingers through her long, untidy hair to give it a semblance of order. 'Oh, all right,' she said, 'I'll go and see who it is – and send them away.' The bell was still ringing intermittently.

As Jan ran downstairs to open the door, Bob skulked in the bedroom, pacing restlessly from side to side, hands thrust in pockets, shoulders hunched. He felt sick with fear. Surely it couldn't be her. For one craven moment he wished he'd never clapped eyes on Jan McLaughlin.

When she opened the door Jan was amazed to see Tamsin standing there, apparently in a state of some distress.

'Oh, Miss McLaughlin,' Tamsin began, 'I'm so sorry. I really am, but I need help. Can you help me, please?'

Jan had a soft heart and so was instantly moved by the sight of poor Tamsin, wide-eyed and white-faced, asking for help. She immediately put her arm round the girl's shoulder and ushered her in, completely forgetting her interrupted pleasures and for the moment oblivious to the presence upstairs of Bob, a prisoner in the bedroom.

Bob stood with the door ajar, straining his ears for the raucous shriek of his wife's voice, but instead he heard Tamsin's unfamiliar tones muttering something to Jan on the way upstairs. He relaxed a little. The worst had not yet happened.

Jan, by now totally absorbed in Tamsin and wanting to know why she should be ringing her geography teacher's doorbell on a Sunday afternoon, almost forgot that Bob was still there. An awareness of his presence lingered somewhere in the back of her mind but did not demand any attention. Had she thought about it, she would have presumed he could just leave without coming into the sitting-room or having anything to do with Tamsin. But he was too frightened to move and so was left for hours to twiddle his thumbs and bite his nails upstairs.

Tamsin had once had a friend who lived in the same street as Miss McLaughlin, which was why she knew where she lived, but it would never normally have entered her head to call, although she liked Jan and thought of her as one of the few decent teachers at school. Now she looked round her at the neat, barely furnished room. Every piece of furniture, all of which was clean-lined and modern, was set at an angle to the wall and on the mantelpiece, between two elongated, carved African heads, was a picture of a little smiling pig with a balloon coming out of its mouth. The pig was saying, 'Thank you for not smoking'. Tamsin, who didn't smoke very much, longed for a cigarette. On one wall was a large, framed reproduction of Millais's painting of Ophelia drowning and on another a poster covered with vivid, multi-coloured, swirling shapes, advertising some charity for the benefit of the mentally ill.

For a fraction of a second Tamsin hesitated. She wondered if she really could say what it was that she had come to say. But she was desperate and had to find some way out of her troubles. This one seemed foolproof.

Jan McLaughlin had long dreaded that one of her pupils would one day come to her with just such a story as Tamsin told her that afternoon, and although she knew what her statutory duty would be under the circumstances, she doubted her ability to deal with the emotions that such a revelation would be bound to arouse. After she had left home, her mother had remarried and her own little sister had been abused in Dundee by a drunken stepfather who was now in gaol. Consequently, Jan felt particularly sensitive on the subject. When she thought of the dreadfully wicked men involved in such dark midnight deeds, her sensible liberal views went to the wall. She thought such men should be flogged, castrated, hanged, imprisoned for life, given no mercy.

Tamsin told her tale beautifully with just the right degree of stress and the right amount of reticence. She gave no horrifying detail, she paused in all the right places, looked at the ground, played it cool.

Too hurt to show much emotion, Miss McLaughlin thought.

'I didn't really realise what was happening at first,' Tamsin said innocently. 'And you see, I love Dad – it's not that I don't love him.' She looked down modestly and played with the fringe of her scarf. Her performance was superb.

How, Miss McLaughlin wondered, could anyone love a man who was capable of such things? She felt stirrings of violent hatred and rage within her but knew that she must control herself. She told herself over and over again in her head the oft-repeated dictum that the abuser is usually a victim himself. To her way of thinking, that was hardly an excuse and certainly not anything she could understand or sympathise with, but she was trying to be reasonable.

'I don't want Dad to get into trouble,' Tamsin was saying. 'It's just that I had to tell someone, you see, because I'm always staying away from school. Sometimes I just get to hate myself so much I can't face going out and then I make all these excuses – and there's this awful thing about the broken window and the onion and the builder – and I can't produce a receipt . . .' Tamsin just wanted Miss McLaughlin to have a quiet word in her form teacher's ear; then, she felt, all would be forgotten and forgiven and she would be able to get on with her life. They'd be sorry for her and understanding and they'd leave her alone and stop talking about truancy and then she'd feel all right and if she started working now, she might still be just in time to pass her exams.

'I think you have been a very brave girl telling me about this,' Miss McLaughlin said collectedly. 'I know how difficult it must have been for you, but I have to tell you that it is my statutory obligation to inform the Social Services.'

Tamsin didn't want the Social Services informed; she didn't want anyone informed apart from her form teacher so, as Miss McLaughlin spoke, with a sudden flash of terror she momentarily glimpsed the terrifying chain of events that she might have unleashed. She began to cry.

Miss McLaughlin, who was in her late thirties, had spent the whole of her adult life as a teacher, and so had some experience of hysterical teenagers, but Tamsin was something quite new. She could not begin to think how to calm her, what to say to her, or indeed what to do with her. She thought that the best thing would be for Tamsin to go home to her mother – she was prepared to accompany her there – and then to come and see her in school in the morning, by which time she would have been able to think the matter over and talk to her colleagues before contacting Social Services.

But the last thing Tamsin wanted was to be accompanied back home to her mother who would surely have some questions to ask. Through her sobs, she swore that Annie was away and wouldn't be back till the following day – if she went home alone her father might come round and she feared she would not have the strength to refuse to let him in.

Miss McLaughlin was horrified. There was no alternative but to harbour Tamsin for the night, unwise though she felt that to be.

'You'll have to sleep on the settee,' she said. 'Will you be all right there? My sister's slept on it. She says it's okay.' Miss McLaughlin somehow felt that to have mentioned her sister was dreadfully tactless, but surely Tamsin could hardly be expected to know what had happened to her.

Tamsin stood up and, as she stifled a few extra sobs, glanced around her. The sofa looked comfortable enough. In the corner next to where she had been sitting was a large teddy bear.

'Ted'll keep you company,' Miss McLaughlin said.

Tamsin was worried neither about the sofa nor about the bear; she was just wondering how she was going to kill the hours until bedtime. The whole thing might be going to get rather heavy but she was confident enough in her charm and in her dramatic ability to be certain that in the end she would be able to persuade Jan McLaughlin not to go to the Social Services. That would spoil everything and only add to her problems.

Jan stood up too. She came over to Tamsin and once again put her arm around her shoulder. It was not easy because Tamsin was far the taller of the two. Jan looked earnestly up into her pupil's face. 'Don't worry,' she said. 'We'll take care of you. I understand how you feel.'

I bet you don't, Tamsin thought bitterly as she looked at the tiny figure beside her, wondering how anyone could be so thin. It struck her then that women like Miss McLaughlin oughtn't to wear jeans; her whole pelvis looked like a wishbone and if she stood with her legs together, you could see the air between her thighs.

A beautiful girl, Miss McLaughlin was thinking. What a tragedy that such a young life should have been so brutally blighted. Men were a terrible breed. And then she suddenly remembered Bob upstairs. She looked at her watch. Oh God! He had been waiting there for hours. She was sure she hadn't heard him leave.

'I say, Tamsin,' she said. 'Will you be all right for a minute or two? I have to go upstairs.' She pointed with her right index finger at the ceiling as she looked up questioningly at Tamsin.

'By the way, Camilla, have you heard about Patrick?'

'Patrick? No. What about Patrick?'

'Well, perhaps I shouldn't say ... You won't tell anyone will you?'

'Fanny, you know I won't. Besides, who on earth do I know who would be remotely interested in anything about Patrick?'

'I don't know. But, I just think it would be better not to say.'

'I never knew you were such a close confidante of Patrick's anyway.'

'I'm not. It's just that Sarah met him in the street and – well – it's rather awful really.'

'Why? What on earth's the matter?'

'Well, apparently – according to Sarah – he was bright red in the face and looked utterly miserable. He sort of whispered in her ear – it was really embarrassing. You know how ghastly Patrick can be – especially when he pushes his face into yours. Really close. You know. Anyway, he told her he had cancer. Prostate ... terrible, isn't it?'

'How dreadful! Poor Patrick. I mean, he's a frightful man, but one really wouldn't wish that on one's worst enemy.'

'I know. Well, I'm not absolutely certain that he actually said cancer – but it does sound like it, don't you think?'

'It does rather, I'm afraid. And what's the news about Tamsin? Has she turned up?'

'Oh – Tamsin – I simply can't find out what's going on there. . . .'

X

When Annie rang Tamsin's school on the Monday morning to find out if they had any news of her daughter or if Tamsin was, indeed, there, the school secretary was extremely unhelpful. Her mind was on other things because that very morning there was to be a visit from the casting director of a new major television film to be made of *Romeo and Juliet*. It was to be a star-spangled production with the old Capulets and Montagues, the nurse and Friar Laurence all played by household names – great classic actors – whilst the younger characters were to be 'unknowns'. The secretary's sixteen-year-old son had recently given what was generally agreed to be an outstanding performance as the young lead in a school production of Peter Shaffer's *Equus*, and she, not unnaturally on that particular morning, could think of nothing but her darling, exquisitely fashioned boy and how he was bound to be chosen to play Romeo if only he would take her advice, talk nicely and brush his hair. Having brought him up on her own since he was two years old she thought of him as entirely her own creation.

'Do leave me alone, Mum,' he'd said as he poured a mountain of cornflakes into a bowl that morning. 'I haven't got a chance in hell of getting the part.' He tossed his head nonchalantly and clenched his jaw muscles, much surer in fact than his mother of success. He was quite confident that the part was all but in his pocket.

So, with such things on her mind, the secretary could hardly remember Tamsin's name or what class or year she was in, or who her form teacher was, but she did promise to try to find out and to ring Annie back later.

Eventually, just before midday, Annie received a rather strange call from Jan McLaughlin of whom she had heard Tamsin speak from time to time. At least it was not another man spouting obscenities on the end of the line, but mixed with an overwhelming relief at the knowledge that Tamsin was safe, Annie felt a terrible sense of dread creep over her; dread that some quite unimaginable horror was about to swamp her and take away her peace of mind for ever.

At first she couldn't quite make out what was being said. Why had Tamsin spent the night with her teacher when her mother was at home and expecting her? Tamsin had known perfectly well that she, Annie, would be home early on Sunday evening. Jan McLaughlin went on talking about the poor child having everybody's sympathy and about what a lot of courage it must have taken for her to talk to someone and about statutory duties and what a difficult time it was going to be for everybody.

When Annie finally put the telephone down she felt utterly shell-shocked. It was unimaginable that Henry was guilty of abusing his daughter and it was equally unimaginable that Tamsin could have gone and told a teacher that he was. Annie knew that her daughter had a fertile mind, and that she suffered from that most terrible of teenage afflictions, the desire to draw attention to herself by shocking. One of the ways she often chose to do this was by inventing the most fantastical lies. She also knew that Tamsin had got herself into a terrible habit of lying whenever it seemed convenient and she felt the need to avoid some issue or other. Above all, Annie felt sorry for Tamsin but, as usual, she was completely at a loss as to how to help her to see the folly of what she was doing. Annie had always been afraid that because of her lies Tamsin would one day land herself in awful trouble; but this – despite all the unfounded gossip which had sprung from God only knew where – was worse than anything she had ever dreamt of. After the Social Services would surely come the police and then poor old Henry would be arrested and even if Tamsin took back what she had said, they'd probably believe her original story and Henry would be sent to prison.

Miss McLaughlin had taken Tamsin to school to see her form teacher before letting her go home to talk to her mother. Jan just wanted to oil the wheels.

Annie waited, sick with dread, and while she waited the telephone rang again. This time it was a very pleasant and polite lady from the Social Services, saying that it was a matter of some urgency that someone should come round and see Tamsin. Would it be convenient to call later that afternoon? Annie said it would. There seemed to be little point in putting off the evil hour.

By the time Tamsin eventually arrived, Annie's shock was beginning to wear off and what had been relief was turning to anger. How dared Tamsin cause such terrible trouble! How dared she tell such heedless lies! Then, in her mind, Annie began to blame Tamsin for everything that had ever gone wrong. She adored her daughter but no one had ever caused her such anguish nor had been so selfishly ungrateful. She felt like jolly well telling Tamsin all that as soon as she arrived. And what about these obscene telephone calls that Annie had been getting this morning? Suddenly she thought that Tamsin must know something about them too, not that she could begin to imagine how they might be explained. And what had Tamsin been up to all the time she was playing truant; why didn't Annie know? Then she started to blame herself for her total inadequacy as a mother. The only person it did not occur to her to blame was Henry. He, she knew, was a pompous ass. But innocent. Of that she was sure.

Annie heard Tamsin's key in the lock and then she heard the front door shut with such a terrific bang that all the walls of the house seemed to shake. She came half upstairs from the kitchen where she was and called to Tamsin, 'Thank God you're back, where on earth do you think you have been? You might have rung. I was sick with worry all last night . . .' Then she saw her daughter's face.

'Tamsin, darling, are you all right? What is it?'

Tamsin had just walked through the front door, thrown her bag to the floor and then, as she glanced at her mother's furious face, she let out a great wail, slumped down on the stairs, buried her head in her arms and began to sob. Finally everything had got totally out of hand, she had no idea what to do and had completely lost confidence in her own ability to sort things out or to sidle out of trouble. Only Annie could help now and she would be horrified when she heard what trouble they were all in.

It was time at last for Tamsin to come clean. In fact she had no alternative and she realised it. So out it all came in garbled, incoherent sentences between the sobs. Out came everything about Billy and about the chat line, about the truancy, the lies, the fear of failing all her exams, about India and the gossip and why she had gone to see her father at the weekend, and out came her anger with Henry, her hatred of Angie, her desperate desire to sort things out for herself and then came the explanation of why she had gone to see Miss McLaughlin – she hadn't at that point cared what she said about Henry because she was so angry with him, but it had never occurred to her that what she told Miss McLaughlin need ever go any further. She had just seen it as a way out of trouble and now she was terrified that Henry would land in prison because of her – and she might as well be dead. Out it all came.

As she spoke, Tamsin gradually became calmer, and as she became calmer, she began to express herself more coherently, and as she became more coherent, it occurred to her to be surprised by her mother's reaction to all this awful news. She had expected Annie to be either very shocked or very angry and yet she appeared to be neither. She just seemed to accept what she heard quite calmly without passing judgement.

In fact, Annie was heartily relieved to be allowed at last to know what was going on so that she might at least have some chance of helping to sort it out. Nothing that she heard pleased her very much, but at least it clarified the situation.

As far as Billy was concerned, all he needed to be told was that Tamsin had no wish to see him again; now that she had explained everything to her mother she surely had the calm and the courage just to write to him or to telephone him and tell him. Annie had no compunctions about Billy's feelings and nor, apparently, did Tamsin. It was just a question of doing the deed. Tamsin would then immediately feel much better.

What did make Annie very angry was the sex chat line but she was determined not to show her anger to Tamsin who, she thought, had been used in the most vile and odious fashion. She also thought that Tamsin had been a complete idiot and she found it hard to understand how on earth she had managed to allow herself to get involved in anything quite so sordid. As far as payment was concerned, Annie considered it was just as well that none had been forthcoming as she hated the idea of Tamsin gaining any benefit at all out of the whole despicable business. It was a foolish, youthful mistake to be put down to bitter experience and forgotten as soon as possible – or at any rate filed away in the dark recesses of the mind. Annie herself undertook to ring British Telecom instantly to tell them that she refused to have the chat-line number – which, of course, Tamsin didn't even know – diverted to her number. She wasn't sure what to do about the character called Dirk but she would have liked to have him stripped naked and pilloried on Hyde Park Corner. For a long time to come she was to hold imaginary conversations with Dirk in her head which always ended with her never being able to find anything quite scathing enough to say to him.

In fact when Annie did ring British Telecom, she found them to be amazingly unhelpful. No one had ever thought of a problem arising from unwanted calls being diverted into someone's house and there was therefore no procedure for preventing them.

'We suggest', said a bright, helpful young woman with adenoids, 'that you go round to their number and ask for the calls not to be redirected any more.' Then, as what seemed like an afterthought, she added, 'But I suppose they could always redirect them back to you again anyway.' Annie spent what seemed like an eternity holding on and listening to cheap music interrupted by dalek voices apologising for keeping her waiting while the bright young adenoidal lady made endless further enquiries. She came back eventually to suggest that the only solution would seem to be for Annie to field the calls as they came in and redirect them back to the other number.

Annie couldn't believe the idiocy of a situation whereby British Telecom was re-routing obscene telephone calls into her house at regular intervals against her will. She told Tamsin that she would just have to get in touch with Dirk and tell him to do something about it, an injunction which brought a fresh burst of tears from Tamsin who swore that that was impossible as Dirk never answered his telephone and in any case she would be sick if she ever had to have anything to do with him ever again in her life. She wished he would die and be eaten by rats, a suggestion which in Annie's view did nothing towards solving the problems in hand.

In fact the line was not due to be switched through again for several days so Annie decided to shelve the matter for the moment and turn her attention to what she regarded as the far more serious affair of Tamsin's accusations of Henry. If the worst came to the worst she would just have to change her telephone number, which would be a great nuisance. Now she had to think about the imminent arrival of the Social Services and of what Tamsin was going to tell them.

Tamsin, with a sudden, untypical burst of energy, strengthened no doubt by her mother's calm practicality, decided on the spur of the moment to ring Billy and to tell him there and then that it was all over between her and him and her and the chat line. In fact, what she did was to leave a message to that effect on his parents' ansaphone, which gave her enormous satisfaction and a fresh burst of adrenalin to face the next obstacle. With the extraordinary optimism of youth she felt that she had dealt with Billy and that that episode in her life was well and truly behind her. What she did not know was that, if not exactly mentally unstable, Billy had a personality disorder which made it peculiarly difficult for him ever to come to terms with not getting his way and which manifested itself in violent outbursts of uncontrollable rage.

Later that afternoon when Annie, apparently totally calm, went to the door to welcome Paula Green from the Social Services, she happened to notice a young man of remarkable beauty standing on the pavement opposite, staring at her front door. In fact, she was feeling so tense at the time and was so concerned to make a good impression on her visitor, that she only half registered what she saw, not wondering for a moment why the beautiful young man with the pony-tail should be staring at her so aggressively.

Tamsin was furious. She didn't want to see anyone from the Social Services. She hadn't wanted them brought in in the first place. None of it was any of their business and she would refuse to talk to them. She thought it was pretty good cheek them thinking they could just come barging round and walking into anyone's house whenever they felt like it. Why weren't they concerning themselves with things which really mattered like all these battered babies?

'Probably', Annie said sharply, 'because the parents of the battered babies didn't see why the Social Services should come barging in on them.' She tried to reason with Tamsin, telling her that the best thing to do would be to come clean, to apologise for what she had done and to hope that the matter would rest there. No one wanted all this upheaval less than Annie did, and if they weren't careful, the police would be called in next. Tamsin was not convinced by her mother's arguments. To act dumb, she thought, would be the best way out. She wasn't prepared for a cosy chat and neither did she wish to expose herself in any way.

Just as Paula Green from the Social Services was making her first kindly, tentative overtures to a sulky Tamsin, who was clearly preparing to be truculent and as uncooperative as possible, there was a terrible thundering on the front door. Then the bell started to ring relentlessly and the shouting started.

For some reason or another, as the thundering increased and as Annie turned to hurry to the door, a picture of the angry young man with a pony-tail flashed into her mind. In an instant she realised it must be Billy – or worse still, Dirk . . . She was not sure that she should open the door at all, but how on earth was she to get rid of this uncontrolled creature?

Patrick was having a field day opposite. He had for some time been watching Billy as he pounded up and down the street and had noticed how he stopped to glare when Annie politely opened the door to someone who appeared to be a stranger to her. Certainly Patrick had never seen Paula Green before and he usually recognised anyone who came to Annie's door. He couldn't quite make her out; she looked all right, he supposed, but something about her demeanour proclaimed hers to be a professional visit rather than a social one. Or so Patrick thought. There was something rather manly and matter-of-fact about her dress and her manner. She didn't quite fit Patrick's idea of what Annie's friends usually looked like.

Not long after the door shut behind this mysterious caller, the young man with the pony-tail suddenly stormed across the road, leaped up the steps and began battering violently on Annie's door. Then he began to shout obscenities. 'Fucking this' and 'Fucking that', and something or other about Tamsin and whores and slags and arseholes all echoing down the street. Patrick had lived in the street for nearly thirty years, but he had never heard or seen anything like it. Well there had been Isabel's husband's suicide which had set the neighbourhood alight

– but nothing quite like this. Patrick was glued to his window.

Meanwhile Annie, inside her house – if only Patrick could have seen through walls – was rather at a loss. There had been Paula Green talking about multi-agencies and Family and Child Protection Units and wanting to take Tamsin and her mother along there for a joint interview with the police, and there had been Tamsin sulking and refusing to speak and then Paula had rashly and unwisely said something about medical examinations and Annie had thought Tamsin was going to hit her and then all of a sudden there had been this terrific banging and shouting.

Annie looked nervously over her shoulder at Paula and Tamsin who had followed her to the door. Paula, in her bomber jacket and slacks and lace-up shoes, had short, dark, curly hair and, Annie thought, an intelligent, good-looking but rather hard face. Tamsin stood just behind her, waving her arms, alive again suddenly.

'Don't let him in, Mum,' she urged. Then, 'Get lost, Billy, can't you?' she shouted almost hysterically at the closed door.

A string of expletives were hurled back from outside with threats to 'break your fucking house down'.

Left to her own devices, Paula, who had no idea what to make of the situation, would probably have opened the door and in her calm, authoritative manner asked the young man to move along. And he would probably have gone, mumbling and grumbling and thinking that he had scored a point. But Annie, like Tamsin, was not in the least inclined to open the door, although at the same time she had a feeling that it might be the only way of quietening the young man down.

'If you don't go away at once,' she said, 'I'll call the police.' She was sticking her heels in. It angered her to think that someone could force their way, unwanted, into her house by use of violence and foul language, and for a moment she didn't even mind what Patrick and all the neighbours thought or said. For all she cared they could hear it all. They had caused enough trouble with their tongues already. They could hardly make matters worse. Tamsin, she suddenly realised, would never ever have thought of accusing Henry in the way she had, if the idea had not been put in her head by that silly child India, and India, of course, would never have spoken as she did if she hadn't listened to the gossips and believed everything they said and revelled in that belief.

Annie wanted a chance to explain all this quite calmly to Paula and for her to believe it and go away. But she had it in mind that Paula would not be quite so easy to shake off. The ball had been set rolling.

It was no good people saying that gossip didn't matter, that no one ever quite believed it, that it was all innocent fun. Annie imagined Tamsin aged fifty and people occasionally whispering about her, about what hadn't happened years ago and about how it had happened. As for Henry, people would never look at him in the same way again – always doubting, always wondering – had he? Hadn't he?

Suddenly the thundering on the door stopped and from the house opposite Patrick saw Billy turn, run down the steps and then disappear into the area outside Annie's kitchen. He couldn't see, however hard he craned his neck, what happened next, but despite the cold weather, he had opened his window a little better to hear the shouted obscenities. Now what he heard was a tremendous shattering of glass.

From inside the house, Annie and Paula and Tamsin heard the same thing.

'Quick!' Tamsin sounded quite hysterical now. 'He'll be climbing in the kitchen window. I don't want to see him.' She stood still in the passage as Annie followed by Paula hurried past her down to the kitchen.

In the event it was not the police but an ambulance that Annie found herself calling. She reached the kitchen to find shattered glass everywhere and, standing outside in the area, stunned by what he had just done, stood Billy pouring blood from both lacerated arms.

'You'd better come in and sit down,' she said gently, as she unlocked the door. 'I'll call an ambulance.'

The ambulance was not long in coming and as it stopped outside Annie's house, Patrick stepped cheerfully out of his own front door, crossed the street, elbows up, eyes bright with concerned interest, reaching the other side just in time to catch the paramedics as they hopped down onto the pavement. 'Spot of trouble?' he addressed them earnestly, one eyebrow raised, neck thrust forward.

He remained there, hovering around the scene until poor, bleeding Billy was bundled into the back of the vehicle and driven away to hospital. Thus he was rewarded with a chance to assure Annie of his ever-readiness to help.

'If there's anything I can do – anything at all,' he urged, 'you know where to find me.' He waved a hand in the general direction of his own front door.

Annie scowled at him. 'There's nothing you can do at all,' she said sharply as she turned to go back inside to face Paula Green and Family and Child Protection Units and Tamsin. Forcing its way all the while between everything else, was the growing awareness of her need for Walter and the realisation that only a very short time remained until Will's return. Tomorrow was it? Or the next day? She shook her head in confusion as if to rid herself of some incubus.

Patrick walked off down the road wondering if he would bump into Sarah or Isabel or someone. Annie's friends, he felt, ought to know that she really was in trouble now. From his minute observation of the afternoon's events, he had been able to deduce that Billy was a drug dealer to whom Tamsin owed money and that Paula was a plain-clothes police officer. He couldn't think why he hadn't realised that at once. Masculine sort of woman.

Sarah was still feeling angry and hurt and unconsidered. No one thought about her or wondered what it felt like to be her – they were all so busy thinking about themselves. Neil – Annie – Isabel – Walter – they were all the same. Selfish, the whole lot of them. It was all right for them; they all had jobs and things to do and self-confidence and plenty of money. What did they have to worry about? For the moment she had quite forgotten that Annie had rung her only that morning to ask for her help over quashing the rumours about Tamsin. All she could think about now was how disagreeable Annie had been about gossip. What a lot of rubbish she'd been talking! Something about gossip shaping the world. What rot! And the very suggestion that she, Sarah, might have been gossiping about her friends! Of course Sarah talked to Isabel and Fanny and people but that was because she was concerned.

The trouble with most of her friends, she was sure, was that they were too selfish. She remembered an aunt saying to her when she was a teenager that happy people were never selfish. She'd thought it rather an odd thing to say at the time, but now she realised that her aunt had been quite right. You only had to look at Walter and Annie. Miserable pair. And as for Neil – funny thing – it had never ever even occurred to her before to wonder whether or not Neil was happy. Well he couldn't be, the way he went on, could he? Neil really was selfish. Look at the way he had refused to think about anything but his own problems at breakfast that very morning. Boring on about Japanese businessmen as if the whole world were interested in them.

She strolled to the window and stared crossly out, bored and wondering how to fill the rest of the afternoon until Neil came home. She'd read the paper – there was nothing of any interest in it. There never was. She'd begun to watch a video of *A Fish Called Wanda* but it hadn't made her laugh at all so she'd turned it off. The trouble with all these films was that they were never any good on video once you'd seen them on the big screen. She wished she'd never bought *A Fish Called Wanda*; she'd certainly never look at it again, although the boys might, she supposed. A bit of a waste of money all the same. She looked disconsolately at the pile of once-watched, or once–half-watched videos on the stand underneath the television and for a moment she hated everything and everybody. Why couldn't they even make better films?

She glanced at the time. She ought to pay some bills, but they could wait; or she could start to peel potatoes for supper, but it was far too early for that. There was a pile of ironing needing to be done in the kitchen, but she was too tired to do it and her back was aching. Perhaps she might ring a friend for a chat but she was fed up with all her friends. Well, she'd just ring Walter's number anyway. She rang it, knowing that he would be at work and as soon as she heard his voice on the ansaphone she rang off. She went idly across to the window again and stared glumly out at the empty street. Even the street was boring. She thought about Will and decided that Annie was being very unfair on him and that she ought to know what people were thinking and saying about her. She went back to the telephone and rang Annie's number this time.

When Annie answered, sounding rather distraught, she suddenly realised that she didn't really have anything to say, so she rang off again.

Back at the window, she was wondering whether she could be bothered to go upstairs and wash her hair when suddenly around the corner came Patrick. She couldn't stick Patrick at the best of times, but even someone you couldn't stick was better than no one when you'd hardly spoken to anyone all day. Anyway, for all his faults, Patrick was full of information, he always had some amusing little tidbit to pass on. She watched him approaching and noticed as he did so, that he had a peculiarly aggravating expression on his face, proud as one who alone knew the secret of the universe. His lower lip was curled out under his top teeth, pressing up hard against them, his mouth turned up at the edges and his brow furrowed. Every muscle in his face seemed to be tensed.

Sarah wondered what could be preoccupying him so. She decided to dash out on the pretext of having forgotten something at the shops, so as to bump into him and hear the latest. At least Patrick would provide an interlude in the monotony of the long day and there might even be a funny story in it with which she could regale Camilla or even Annie. For the moment she had put her irritation with Annie out of her mind.

She dashed to the hall and grabbed a coat and her front door keys and was in the street in no time, but unfortunately Patrick had been walking fast and so had passed her house already and was walking away from her up the street. In order to bump into him she would somehow have to overtake him and turn round. So she was hurrying along, half walking, half running, holding her breath and about to cross the road, better to execute her plan, when she suddenly saw Walter appear round the corner on the opposite pavement. She didn't want to see

Walter at all for complicated reasons which she herself would have found hard to understand. Besides, seeing him at this hour, when she was convinced he should still be at work, instantly made her suspicious. He was obviously up to something – with Annie no doubt. They were probably going somewhere together. She turned her head and refused to look in Walter's direction and not wanting now to cross the road, she was obliged to slacken her pace and drop behind Patrick again.

Walter was quite simply coming home early from work for once. He had no guilty secret, no ulterior motive and nothing very much on his mind except for the sweet thought of Annie. As he rounded the corner he glanced across the street and saw Patrick on the other side, walking towards him with his usual urgency. Sarah was scuttling along behind him in a most peculiar fashion, looking out of place and almost guilty as she suddenly turned her face away, apparently not wanting to acknowledge Walter.

But, on seeing Walter, Patrick quickened his pace. He darted out across the street.

'Ah, Walter,' he said, 'I'm so glad to see you. I think you are one who ought to know. There's been a little trouble in the street . . .' And so he began his saga.

Sarah pretended not to have noticed anything and, as Walter turned for a moment from Patrick to wave at her, she strode on up the street and out into the Bayswater Road, consciously and intentionally cutting her old friend dead.

That evening she telephoned Isabel who was out and Camilla and Fanny whose lines were both engaged for hours, and so eventually had to make do with telling Neil, when he got in rather late for supper, that Walter was definitely up to no good with Annie. Why else would he have been in the street in the middle of the afternoon? She didn't tell Neil that she had cut Walter. She felt a little

172

uncomfortable about that although, of course, she had been in a hurry at the time and wouldn't have had time to stop and talk.

Neil didn't appear very interested – perhaps he was still thinking about Japanese businessmen. In fact he was thinking of his personal life and feeling rather unsettled, but he was a controlled man whose emotions were usually only to be guessed at behind a distant manner which under stress became distracted. His relationship with Sarah, he knew, was heading nowhere and he was wondering how long it could be sustained in its present unsatisfactory form.

She, of course, was feeling as discontented as anyone would whose only point of interest in the day had been to see a friend returning from work an hour or two earlier than usual.

'Drugs – definitely drugs, according to Patrick.'

'Oh, come on Fanny, when did you ever believe a word Patrick said?'

'Well, you've got to admit that that's what it looks like anyway.'

'Yes, of course. In any case it would hardly be surprising – after all drugs and abuse do go together. It's one of the ways you can tell, you know.'

'But Camilla, what on earth do you think is going to happen next?'

'God alone knows. I should have thought that almost anything could happen. . . .'

XI

'If she's hanging around waiting for Walter to commit himself, she must be wasting her time.'

'But, Camilla, do you really think she'd throw Will over just like that – and for Walter of all people? It'd be a terribly unkind thing to do the minute he got back. And where would he go, poor man?'

'Hotel, I suppose. I know he sold his flat when he took up with Annie.'

'Has he got any family?'

'Y-e-s, I've met a brother, but I think he lives abroad. And he's got some pretty ancient parents. Up in Lincolnshire. His father's a parson.'

'I never knew that. But, anyway, what about Annie?'

'I tell you, there'd be no point in her chucking Will if she was doing it for Walter's sake, but what you don't seem to have taken in, Fanny, is that even without Walter, that relationship's been doomed from the start because Annie's always wanted Will to change his job. She hates him going away – she doesn't like being alone.'

'She's not alone. She's got Tamsin.'

'No, but you know what I mean. In any case they can't have been very happy, what with Will so determined to

174

go on doing what he was doing – anyway Annie was never the right person for him. The only person Will's ever been in love with was Sarah.'

'It would have been a disaster if he'd married her. She would never have put up with him being away all that time, I'm sure.'

'In one way and another, I think Neil's away almost as much.'

'I suppose he doesn't go for such long stretches, though.'

'No, but Sarah's looking pretty fed up, don't you think? I don't really blame her – Neil works so hard. He's always either in his office or at some conference abroad.'

'I wonder what it's like for Will when he gets back. Annie's house must seem very strange after wherever he's been staying.'

'I know. He must feel claustrophobic I should think; her house is so pretty-pretty and cosy. I expect he rather dreads it. In fact I think that part of the reason Will goes on doing that job is because he wouldn't like to be with Annie all the time. If it had been someone else, he'd probably have settled down by now.'

'Yes, I think you're right. But I still don't think it would be very nice of her to welcome him home and then just go off with Walter.'

'I promise you there isn't a chance of that happening. Look at Walter. It's obvious he's terrified of women. I'd be prepared to bet you that he'll never get married again. Or even live with anyone for that matter. You see I think he's a cold fish.'

'Perhaps he is gay like Sarah said. Perhaps he never did have an affair with Isabel – after all, we can't be sure.'

'Oh, I think we can, you know. I mean it was pretty obvious. He's probably bi-sexual – or anything goes . . .'

'Oh dear, I hope they don't all give each other Aids. I

don't suppose Will would have any difficulty in finding someone else, do you? After all, he's quite attractive, don't you think?'

'I'm not sure about that. His eyes are a bit close together for my liking.'

'I don't think so. Anyway, I've never noticed it. He's got a good figure. Looks very young.'

'He's all right. A bit arrogant, though.'

'Which would you rather be on a desert island with, Walter or Will?'

'Oh, Will, any day. Wouldn't you?'

'Definitely. He'd probably be quite good at making log cabins, too, which would be a help.'

'What about Henry?'

'He's very good-looking, but I doubt he'd be much use when it came to log cabins.'

'I should hardly think so, but I couldn't bear to be alone with Henry at all – let alone on a desert island. Mind you, with his proclivity for the young, you'd probably be as safe as houses.'

'It sounds as if Henry's going to end up in prison, the way things are going.'

'I'm sure he will. And have you heard what happened yesterday?'

'What was that?'

'Some drug dealer broke into Annie's house and the police were round there and apparently there was the most terrific shindy. Needless to say, Patrick had his nose glued to the window opposite and saw everything that went on.'

'Oh, yes, I did hear about that. What on earth do you suppose Angie will do when she finds out about Henry?'

'Perhaps she knows already. I certainly think she'd leave him. Apart from anything else, she's got her own child to think about. I wouldn't hang around, would you?

I mean, put yourself in her place – supposing you found out that Brian was doing something to India . . .'

'Camilla, don't be disgusting! How could you say such a thing?'

'No, of course he's not, but just supposing . . .'

'Look here, I must go now, it's getting awfully late and I've got to be somewhere . . . Sorry. 'Bye . . .'

'Hi, Sarah, how're you? It's Camilla.'

'Camilla! Haven't seen you for ages. What've you been up to?'

'Nothing much. I just rang for a chat. Wondered how you were – what's new?'

'I expect you've heard all the latest about Annie and Tamsin and the break-in and all that?'

'Yes, I've just been talking to Fanny actually. She was rather huffy.'

'Fanny, huffy? Why?'

'I don't really know, but I wondered if it might have been – oh, I don't know, perhaps I shouldn't say . . .'

'Shouldn't say what?'

'Well – promise you won't repeat this, will you?'

'Of course I won't say a thing, but what is it?'

'Well, I know it seems ridiculous, I mean I don't really think it's very likely, but there was something about the way she reacted . . . Do you think it just might be possible that – you know – Brian and India . . . ? It would explain why India was so concerned about Tamsin . . .'

Will was weary. He'd been away for almost too long this time and he needed to get home, back to Annie. He was tired of living in a hotel where there was often no water, usually no electricity and where the lavatories didn't work. Above all, he was tired of being afraid. He thought of Annie's quiet presence and longed to be with her.

While he'd been away, Will had had a fling with a French aid worker, a small, dark, wiry woman with short hair, short legs, big brown eyes and a big nose. Martine was strong and brave and matter-of-fact, with her two feet planted firmly on the ground both as far as work was concerned and as far as her relationship with Will was concerned. She knew about Annie and knew that Will loved her. Or rather Will had told her that he loved Annie, but Martine sometimes wondered. Will, she thought, was an adventurer and an egoist who really loved only himself. He didn't seem to miss Annie very much or mind about her welfare. It almost seemed that she was no more than part of a picture that Will wished to paint of himself. As for Martine, she was not in love with Will. She liked him and was attracted to him but she could never really love an Englishman. *Trop poètique*, she thought. Never practical enough.

What Will was looking forward to almost as much as being with Annie was the cosy comfort of her house. He'd let his own flat several years ago when he'd first taken up with Annie. He'd thought of selling it but that seemed foolish as he didn't particularly need the money at the time and, in any case, he liked the idea of keeping it there as a bolt-hole. Will thought he loved Annie. Certainly he was fonder of her and had a greater regard for her than he had ever had for any other woman, but the idea of settling down filled him with horror.

Annie, he thought, could manage. She'd got her daughter and so wasn't desperate for a child. In any case the years were running out for that. She'd got her job, a nice house, family and friends so that even if she did miss him when he was away for so long, it couldn't be all that bad. In any case she struck him as someone who cherished her independence and was quite easy with her own company. Occasionally it crossed his mind to wonder if, during his long absences, she had the odd fling like himself. He thought not. Women were different. And Annie was not that kind of person anyway.

Martine was all right. She'd answered a need and their shared experience of the horrors of war had made a bond. Back in England, Will knew that he would be unable to talk about his experiences to anyone, even to Annie. Even those who followed the foreign news with the greatest interest were quite unable to comprehend what it was really like out there. They would ask questions with eager, alert faces and as soon as you began to answer, their expressions glazed over and you were forced to realise that you and they inhabited different worlds. They turned to talking about trivial domestic matters like the interest rate, the unpopularity of the government, or, worst of all, the state of the monarchy.

Will had come to realise that what he went home for, as much as anything, was repose. For a breath of English insularity, for a gentle woman who cherished him, and even to see his parents; quiet, retired, military folk, people with little imagination and old-fashioned standards who lived in a vicarage in what used to be called Huntingdon-shire where, of course, there was honey still for tea.

Sometimes when Will was away he allowed himself to romanticise about England in the most sentimental way – oh to be in England and all that rubbish – but as soon as he'd been back for a week or two, sipping Chardonnay in W8, he began to feel restless. Worse than restless. Worse than bored. He felt an irresistible desire for danger, a need for the adrenalin which accompanies fear, like a mountaineer or a racing driver seeking ever greater, ever more terrifying challenges.

This time, as usual when he travelled home, he began to wonder if the time hadn't come for him to call it a day. Perhaps now he really would ask Annie to marry him and they would settle down like any other middle-aged, middle-class couple to a cosy parochial life. One major obstacle to such a course of action was Tamsin, though. Will groaned out loud to himself. He didn't really want to share his life with Tamsin. She was too tricky and too selfish, making far too many demands on her mother. Will always thought that Annie indulged her daughter and wondered why on earth she bothered so much about her.

Even so, part of Will was drawn to the idea of settling down, particularly now when he was feeling so war-torn and weary – after all, Tamsin would surely have left home in a year or two. But, with a sickening dread tinged with a reawakening of real fear, another part of him recognised the inevitability of surrender to that old familiar urge. He still needed danger; he knew that. Perhaps in ten years' time he would have had his fill of it and then he would think again.

In order to get back from Sarajevo, Will had wanted to try to hire a car and drive to Zagreb, but friends had dissuaded him, telling him that to do so would be tantamount to suicide, and, since no one had been prepared to go with him, he had finally allowed himself to be persuaded. Even he was eventually ready to admit that there was no need for such folly, so he waited for a lift with a UN convoy going to Split and flew from there to Zagreb. The whole journey seemed to have taken an eternity and now, as the Air Croatia plane was at last circling Heathrow, he looked down at the vast grey agglomeration of London and sort of wished he had never come. It required such a monumental effort to change gear, to re-enter that other life, to forget to be afraid, to presume that the lavatory would flush and that there wouldn't be a sniper round the corner in Notting Hill, that he could hardly bear the thought of it. But then he thought of Annie, of the sweet welcome she always gave him and how happy she would be to see him back and he began to feel impatient for her embrace. She would be there at the airport, of course, anxiously waiting for his plane to land, waiting for the sign to say: 'baggage in hall'.

Two days earlier Walter had decided not to wait any longer. He would have to speak to Annie and tell her that he loved her. Since the crisis of Tamsin's disappearance and reappearance, and since the terrible accusations she had made against Henry, Walter had felt himself growing ever closer to Annie. He sensed that she was beginning to turn to him and to depend on him more and more and he also sensed with a flickering of terrified hope that she was beginning to grow fond of him as well. Perhaps even to love him too.

Walter also sensed that Will and Annie might not be totally happy together – not that Annie had ever discussed hers and Will's relationship with Walter. It was just that she had the forlorn, faraway look of someone who is not entirely happy. It was perfectly obvious that she must be lonely at times – but then perhaps the faraway look was just the look of a rather solitary person. Then again, he told himself, her sadness might come from the fact that she missed Will, and yet, because she didn't mention him that often, Walter somehow doubted this.

It was a long time since Walter had told anyone that he loved them but he realised that if he was to tell Annie at all, it would have to be now, before Will came home. He could hardly do so with Will there, settled in, living with Annie as her partner. Yet his mind was incapable of grasping what the consequences might be were he to speak the truth. He certainly didn't look far into the future and imagine what might happen. He didn't even wonder in any practical way what would be happening in a year's time – or even six months' time. All he could think of was

Annie and how he loved her, wanted her, wanted her with him all the time, and how he dreaded losing her. He feared that she might not reciprocate his feelings, but at one and the same time he was sure that she did. Anything else seemed too difficult to think about.

Of course he should have spoken earlier, long before Will's return. That, he somehow thought, would have been fairer on everyone. Now what would happen? Supposing Annie were to say no, she didn't love him. What then? And then, supposing she were to say yes, she did love him? What would happen then? He was annoyed with himself for having made such a muddle of things. Whatever he did now he would be putting Annie in a difficult position. He dismissed the possibility of waiting for Will to come home and go away again as he surely would. For Walter, the tide was now flowing and could not be turned. He could no longer wait. He would have to speak.

In fact, when Walter thought about Will he began to feel quite angry. He'd always quite liked him, although he hardly knew him; he'd admired his courage and even slightly envied his apparently carefree spirit of adventure, his guts and what had always seemed to be his moral fibre. Will was the sort of man that other men were often wary of because in their heart of hearts they would have liked to have been like him themselves.

But now Walter suddenly saw an arrogant, selfish, egotistical man who certainly didn't deserve the wonderful, beautiful, loyal woman who awaited him. Will looked like a poet, not a journalist, Walter thought with a sudden surge of irritation. The thin, pale, nervous face and fair lank hair, that boyish manner, were all more reminiscent of Siegfried Sassoon or Wilfred Owen than of a hard-headed foreign correspondent. Not that Walter had the faintest idea of what either Sassoon or Owen looked like, but he'd certainly never admired Rupert Brooke's girly profile. Walter's irritation mounted.

It seemed to Walter that Annie had been badly treated by Will, whichever way you looked at it. She was left alone for most of the time, as far as he could see, with no one to support her through her difficulties. It didn't occur to him that after the ordeal of a broken marriage and with a difficult child to bring up, Annie might have been made quite happy by a less demanding, less permanent kind of relationship, might have cherished her independence and enjoyed spells on her own. Perhaps it made it easier for her that Will was not there all the time. And perhaps she loved Will. Walter couldn't bear to think about that. All he could do was to kick himself for not having made a move earlier and all because he thought he had to be gentle-manly – or because he was a coward, or because he was an innocent.

Anyway, now he was in a dreadful muddle because he had to speak, and he had to speak at a moment when Annie was unable to think about anything but Tamsin and Henry and just when she was about to welcome Will back from an arduous stint away.

Yesterday, when he'd come home early from work, he'd met Patrick who was totally delighted by some awful drama which he had witnessed outside Annie's house. He was full of it and insinuated for reasons at which Walter could only too easily guess, that Walter would be especially concerned. He should be the very first person who ought to hear about it all. Meanwhile, Sarah had sidled by, only too obviously cutting Walter dead, probably for the same reasons.

Walter could have been hurt by Sarah's unfriendly behaviour. After all, he had always regarded her as a good friend even though he had been aware of the fact that she could be tricky. Now he was amazed by her and merely thanked his lucky stars that he had never been too closely involved with her. It would have been disastrous. He wondered about her and Will. He also wondered about all the telephone calls he'd been having lately when the caller rang off as soon as he answered. He could never prove that Sarah was responsible for them, but he was ninety-nine per cent convinced that she was. He wondered if she had been plaguing Annie in the same way. She must, he thought, be pretty unhappy. He couldn't see why she should be, though. Neil was a nice man.

As soon as Walter could extricate himself from Patrick, he hurried on home where the first thing he did was to telephone Annie. You couldn't believe everything that Patrick said, but it was perfectly clear that something had been going on.

Annie sounded pretty desperate. She said she had someone there and couldn't talk. Walter wondered if Patrick might be right on this occasion. Perhaps it was the police? Annie wanted to know if he would be in later.

'Sure you're not going out?' she asked, with what appeared to be some urgency.

No, he wasn't going out.

'Will you be there all evening?' The same urgent tone.

Yes, he'd be there all evening.

She'd ring later then, she said and quickly rang off.

Walter sat and waited. He waited for a long time. It seemed to him that he waited for an age – thinking about Annie all the time. He couldn't think what the truth could be about what had really happened, but he knew now that he could wait no longer and so it was at this moment that he decided that he would have to declare himself before Will's return, however imminent that might be.

It was funny to think that his decision might have been precipitated by an encounter in the street with a terrible old gossip. Walter didn't at all like the idea that Patrick might in any way have influenced his fate.

Eventually the telephone rang and Annie was able to tell him what had really happened. She had at last said goodbye to Paula Green, who had had a terrible time trying to persuade Tamsin to talk to her. Tamsin had admitted to her mother that what she had said about Henry was total fabrication but she could not be persuaded to talk to the authorities, although it had now been left that Annie would take her in the morning to what they called the Family and Child Protection Unit to talk to the police and the Social Services. As far as Annie could see, there was no immediate escape from the nightmare. She couldn't bring herself to ring Henry to tell him what had happened, but hoped that Tamsin's denials the next day would be enough to put an end to the affair once and for all, although she dreaded that the police might still feel it incumbent upon them to see Henry.

Annie wanted to see Walter but she must stay with Tamsin and she felt that, under the circumstances, it wouldn't be a good idea for Walter to come round to her house.

'You've been such a help,' she said, 'and I miss you.'

She misses me, Walter thought. She misses me and she's only in the next-door street and I can't see her. At work they were all talking about his forthcoming trip to Mali. No one could understand why he seemed so uninterested in it suddenly. Mali. He didn't want to go to Mali just now.

He rang her later to ask if she was all right and when it would be possible to see her. He felt very cross with Tamsin and even crosser with himself. Time was running out and he was beginning to be desperate for an outcome. Having promised Annie that he would be in all evening, he felt quite restless and pounded up and down the small length of his sitting-room, quite unable to think of anything but what he would say to Annie, unable even to play the piano. By midnight he decided that Annie was unlikely to ring again so, knowing that he wouldn't sleep, he decided to go out for a walk. That night he walked for miles, heedless of where he was going and only returned to bed in the small hours.

Meanwhile Patrick with his prostate problems had been jumping up and down at intervals, tweaking his curtains to look at Annie's house, always wondering who might be coming or going. But he saw no one. Funny. He was surprised at Walter for not going round.

Annie sat at Heathrow waiting for the Air Croatia flight from Zagreb to land. She had arrived in good time only to find that it had been delayed for two hours. She should have rung the airport before leaving home. She couldn't think why she hadn't. Too much on her mind she supposed.

Yesterday morning had been a nightmare. She had spent all morning with Tamsin and the police and the Social Services and blasted Miss McLaughlin had put in an appearance, ready and desirous to believe the worst. Tamsin had had time to think about what had happened and thank goodness had come to the sensible conclusion at last that the best thing to do – in fact the only thing to do – was to tell the truth. She'd spent hours going over and over what had happened and why. She had, Annie felt almost sure, eventually convinced the authorities who, it had to be admitted, had been both patient and kind.

In the afternoon Tamsin decided that she wanted to go back to school. She looked dreadful and had been crying. Annie told her that she should try to put the whole thing behind her. It was, with luck, all over now. But they both knew that there was a possibility that the police might still decide to talk to Henry.

It had been a relief to see Tamsin going off to school. Annie needed a respite after the last two days. As she sank exhausted onto the sofa and put her feet up, she longed for Walter's comforting presence. She had begun to wonder if he loved her and at times felt sure that he did, but was still puzzled by Sarah having stated so categorically that he was gay. Perhaps she was making a fool of herself in her mind. Perhaps she ought to stop thinking about Walter and concentrate instead on Will who would be back any minute. She began to think about gossip again. How dared people go around announcing quite arbitrarily what other people's sexual tastes were and what they thought and why. In the long run, she thought, you never knew a thing about what went on in another person's mind. You hardly knew what went on in your own half the time.

How could anyone even begin to suppose that they understood the dark side of other people, let alone their hopes and fears and disappointments and all the multitude of things which went to make them act as they did. All those gossipy people thought they knew everything there was to know, not only about her and Henry and Tamsin, but about everyone else in the Village for that matter. She hated them for it and suddenly thought she would have to move. But barely had the thought crossed her mind before she realised, with a pang, that she couldn't move away from Walter whether he was gay or not. The other thing about gossip, she thought, was that it always stuck. If not, why did she keep coming back to this nonsense about Walter? And what did it matter to her in any case?

Then, as she dozed on the sofa, the unopened newspaper on her knee, she was suddenly woken by the shrill ringing of the telephone. At first she couldn't think what time of day it was or why she was sleeping on the sofa; then, as she reached for the telephone and, with joy, recognised Walter's voice, she remembered exactly what had been happening.

Walter was about to leave work instantly. He wanted to come round and see her at once.

He came. And he told her he loved her. She told him that she loved him, too, and then she cried because she couldn't see what on earth they could do about it: Will was due home the next day.

They went upstairs and they made love and Walter told Annie that he wanted to marry her. And she cried again and said that she didn't see how on earth it could be, and then they had to get up because Tamsin might come in from school at any moment. And they were just in time, sitting primly in the kitchen drinking a glass of white wine each when Tamsin turned up.

Tamsin looked a great deal brighter than when Annie had last seen her. She was altogether delighted by what had happened that afternoon. So much so that she wasn't even annoyed by the sight of her mother sitting in such cosy intimacy with Walter. She had been to see her headmistress who, it turned out, had been extremely kind and understanding. If Tamsin agreed to attend school regularly and to get back to work at once, then all the past truancy including the episode of the onion and the builder's receipt, all the lies and all the undone work, would be overlooked. But this was a last chance. So, Tamsin thought, it had come right in the end. For the moment she had decided to forget that there might still be trouble brewing with Henry.

Poor girl, the headmistress thought as she dismissed Tamsin. The child deserved another chance. After all, there was no smoke without fire. Just because nothing could be proved, it didn't mean that nothing had happened. The fact that Tamsin had withdrawn her accusation meant very little. After all, something must lie at the root of such delinquent behaviour as Tamsin's.

So Annie was sitting at Heathrow thinking about Walter and thinking about Will in turn, looking ridiculously often at her watch, feeling everything – happy and unhappy, excited, guilty, afraid, sad . . .

She didn't want to make any hurried decisions but she knew she loved Walter and she even thought they could be happy together. Life was short enough and she had known – always known, perhaps – but certainly known for a long time now that she and Will would never really settle down together. There were things about Will which she liked and would always value, but she couldn't support for ever the theory that only he really counted. She thought back over the past and began to feel resentful and even angry at the remembrance of Will's selfishness, inconsiderateness, even of the way that he always had to be the centre of attention. He was always the one, when they went out, whose opinions in a group had to be heard, to whom people – half afraid, perhaps – always deferred. He was the one at home who insisted on coffee rather than tea for breakfast, who chose where they went, whom they saw, what channel they watched on the television. She realised only too well that this was partly her fault, but only partly because if he lived at home all the time, like most people's partners, she was sure she would never have allowed it to happen.

She looked at her watch again and she looked at the television screen announcing arrival times and there was still another interminable half-hour to go before the plane was even due to land. She couldn't bear the thought of Will somewhere up there in the sky, looking at his watch and longing to land, and longing to see her. This, she thought, was going to be one of the hardest things she had ever done in her life but although she knew that Will would be hurt, she couldn't help thinking that somewhere in his make-up there was an element of steel which prevented him from ever really minding anything. He would run his fingers through his lank hair, look at her distantly, accept what she had said and quietly make other arrangements. Then he'd be off again, soon. Danger was the only thing that Will really loved. He was a sort of danger junkie and he'd never give it up. But still the knowledge that she had let him down hurt her and she wanted to say she was sorry and to be forgiven. Besides, they'd had some very happy times and they should never be discounted.

Still, she would have to tell him that things had changed. They could not go on together any more, but not today. Today she would not be able to tell him. It would be too unkind. She'd have to wait – wait till tomorrow or the next day. Apart from everything else, there was all the stuff about Tamsin to tell him – not that he was interested in Tamsin – and questions to ask him about himself. Questions which would probably remain unanswered. And meanwhile, there was Walter . . . Why the hell hadn't Walter said something before and given her time to think?

She glanced at the television screen and nearly jumped out of her skin when she saw that the Zagreb flight had landed. Suddenly it was there. She stood up and began to pace up and down, frowning and tense, oblivious of the crowds around her so that she kept bumping into people as they stood still, hands on their luggage trolleys, gawping fatuously into the air in the hopes of seeing some directions – to a taxi, a bus or the underground.

'Sorry,' she kept saying. 'Oh sorry,' running her hands through her hair in her embarrassment, and hunching her shoulders.

Then someone walking behind her as she dawdled rammed a trolley into her ankle which brought her sharply to her senses.

And now the television screen was saying, 'baggage in hall'. So this was it. Will, who had come back home to nothing, would be here in an instant – coming through that door, running towards her.

Then all at once, there he was, looking just the same as ever – surely nothing had really changed – but thin, even a bit gaunt. As soon as he saw her, his whole face lit up, he dropped the backpack that hung casually from one shoulder carelessly at his feet and opened his arms to embrace her.

Henry was feeling pretty desperate. He'd put the London flat on the market, hoping that that would solve his problems. For the moment it might, but his deteriorating circumstances at Lloyd's made it seem increasingly likely that the house in the country would have to go next. Every year he hoped he'd seen the worst, but he never had. He was sleeping badly and could think of nothing but his financial situation. He realised at the same time that his relationship with Angie was going through a bad patch, but put it down to the fact that women hardly ever understand finance which obviously made it quite out of the question to discuss the matter with her. When he did tell her about the flat, he was pleasantly surprised by how well she took it. He wondered how on earth she would cope if and when the house went. He instinctively felt she would be angry. She had never been very good at accepting defeat.

The latest news about Lloyd's which had come like a bombshell that morning, had quite caused him to put any thoughts about Tamsin out of his mind. Where, he wondered, would he and Angie go? What would they do?

How would he send Matthew to school? Where would he ever get any more money from? For a fleeting moment, as he buried his head in his hands, elbows on his desk, he could almost understand those whom he had always thought of as taking the easy way out. But then, he was a Catholic, so he would never kill himself. He shuddered at the thought. It had made him very cross when a year ago people had insinuated that his aunt, whose body was found in the Tarn, had drowned herself. Of course she would never have done such a thing. In any case, the banks of the Tarn were notoriously slippery.

All the same, Henry had rarely felt so low or so helpless. He didn't know where to turn for help, or for comfort of any kind. Even Father Leatham could be little use in these circumstances.

Angie had taken Matthew, who had at last learned to walk, shopping for shoes and the daily help had gone home, so Henry was alone in the house when the police car drove up. He heard it crunching on the gravel and at first presumed it to be Angie come home, but he looked at his watch and realised that she could hardly be back yet.

He went to the front door and there they were, with their scrubbed faces and pleasant smiles.

Policemen do get younger every day, Henry thought. And as for the WPC, she looked like a child.

When they had established his identity, the WPC said, with a sweet smile, 'We'd like a word with you, Sir, if we may.' And they stepped across the threshold.

'Fanny hallo.'

'Oh Camilla, it's you.'

'I just rang because I felt I rather put my foot in it this morning. You know I was just gabbling – of course I didn't mean what I said.'

'Said? About what?'

'Oh, nothing really. I just had the feeling that I'd sort of offended you.'

'Of course you didn't, don't be ridiculous. What are you doing tomorrow by the way? We might have lunch.'

'Yes, that'd be really nice. Will you come here? Or shall we go out?'

'You come here. I'm inviting you.'

'Okay, lovely. Thanks. And I'll tell you then what I've heard about Henry and Angie.'

'Henry and Angie? What on earth can you have heard about them? By the way, did you realise that Will came home today?'

'Yes, I thought it was today. What happened?'

'I don't really know. Annie went to the airport and Patrick saw them when they got back. They looked pretty cheerful, according to him.'

'Annie's not going to say anything, is she? She's got nothing to lose by just keeping quiet. I can't really say I blame her, can you?'

'I don't know. I'll never really be able to make Annie out.'

'I don't think there's anything particular to make out. It's easy to see what she thinks. Bit callous really – out for herself . . .'

XII

Angie had hardly turned a hair when she learned that Henry was having to sell the London flat because, despite the fact that he refused to discuss his problems with her, she was already half expecting it. She could tell that he was worried and of course she knew he was deeply involved in Lloyd's. She had almost reached the point of making up her mind to leave if and when it came to selling the country house. Poverty had certainly not been part of the bargain when she married Henry. She was someone whom poverty would never suit and so had certainly never taken all that stuff about 'for richer, for poorer' too seriously. After all, you could only be expected to put up with so much. On the other hand, if Henry didn't have to sell the house she would probably stay. Henry would need her there, and then, of course, it was her home. Under those circumstances she supposed she would look for a lover. Her relationship with her husband was heading nowhere and without realising it, she was afraid. In order to believe in her own reality she had a need to see herself reflected in the eyes of an admirer; someone who existed for her alone and whose existence confirmed her own.

So she was beginning in a sly little way to look around

for somewhere else to lay her head, or at least for someone else to care for her. She knew she was a pretty woman and she supposed that there must be a few dissatisfied men around looking for an escape route from their own ill-conceived marriages. But she would bide her time. She had made a mistake once and she had no intention of making another. If it came to leaving, the wrench would be great when it came to the garden. She certainly hoped it wouldn't come to that.

She was thinking along these lines as she drove back home with Matthew for whom she had bought no shoes. The baby had howled in the shop and wrinkled up his toes, refusing to allow his feet to be forced into the sensible little shoes produced by the shop assistant for him to try. He had wriggled and squirmed and his nose had run and his cries had become shriller and shriller until he finally threw himself on the floor and held his breath for what seemed like an eternity. Angie could have hit him and probably only managed to restrain herself on account of the shop girl's presence. Eventually, unable to tolerate his behaviour any longer, she snatched him up roughly and carried him off, screaming, to the car where she strapped him into his car seat and threatened him with never ever having any shoes. When he was older he would have to walk to school barefoot and his feet would get cold and he'd cut them on stones and everyone would laugh at him.

As soon as Angie set out for home, the motion of the car lulled Matthew to sleep and she was left to get on with her own thoughts. Mothering was not really for her although sometimes she felt quite fond of Matthew and even proud of him, but when he behaved badly she found her patience running out all too quickly and then she longed to be able to turn her back on her child. One advantage of leaving Henry would be that she would only have

Matthew for half the time under which circumstances, she persuaded herself, she would be an altogether better parent. It pleased her to think of Henry having to take Matthew shopping. Then he would know what it was like – what she had to put up with.

She wondered if Henry would make a better father to a son than he had to his daughter. Not with all his twisted Catholicism, she thought. Then she began to think about Tamsin whom she disliked so cordially. She didn't regard Henry as being a good father to her – certainly the relationship between the two was evidence of there being something deeply wrong somewhere – and yet, it couldn't be denied that Henry loved his daughter in his way. It made Angie very angry to see how tense and anxious Henry became whenever Tamsin was expected and how buttoned up and withdrawn he became when they quarrelled which they usually did. It annoyed her to notice Henry's pride in what Angie regarded as Tamsin's brash good looks. They wouldn't last. Angie even thought that Henry was sometimes half attracted to his daughter, which she found galling and rather disgusting.

She reached home just as the two police officers were leaving. It occurred to her that they smiled at her in a somewhat patronising way as they climbed into their car – pitying even.

'What on earth were they doing here?' she wanted to know.

Henry was completely shattered by what had just happened so that at first he found it hard to speak, let alone to tell Angie what it was that the police had called about. In fact, he didn't really want to tell her. The suggestion that he had been molesting his own daughter was so revolting and so preposterous that it would be better if the whole matter were forgotten, never to be alluded to again. Luckily, Tamsin had retracted her vile accusations and there was nothing for the police to do but to go away and get on with the proper business of catching criminals. They were not going to press charges, they told him grandly, and in slightly threatening tones.

But why, they had wanted to know, would a young girl tell a story like that about her own father if there was no truth in it? The inference was that she had retracted it out of fear of the consequences.

Henry was very angry indeed. How could his own child have behaved so wickedly? Why had she done it? He felt like going straight to London and shaking her till her teeth rattled in her head. And then behind the anger he felt hurt and betrayed. He did not deserve this on top both of Lloyd's and of Angie's gradual withdrawal.

He had been quietly controlled with the police officers but now, here was Angie wanting to know what had been happening, standing there in front of him, looking almost accusing herself. The thought flitted across his mind that Annie would have been kinder. More understanding at least.

But as Henry looked at Angie standing there indignantly questioning him, he decided that he would tell her about the police. After all, he had nothing to hide, nothing to be ashamed of; perhaps when she heard what had been happening she might even direct her anger against the police — more probably at Tamsin — and champion her husband for a change. He needed her strength to be on his side. For once it wasn't Father Leatham he wanted.

Angie, whose mind had been totally preoccupied with Lloyd's and pennilessness and the possibility of losing her home, was amazed when she heard what Henry had to tell her. Her first reaction was indeed to be angry with Tamsin. How dared she invent such horrible lies? Did she begin to realise what the consequences might have been of her actions? Even if no more was said, people would hear about what had happened and some of them would always wonder about the truth and forever look at Henry through new, accusing eyes. She glanced down at him sitting on the sofa with his head in his hands. It seemed as if he was about to cry. She felt slightly sick. Why couldn't he stand up, put his shoulders back, shake it off, get on with life?

'Why don't you go and see Father Leatham?' she asked with a faint sneer in her voice. 'You usually seem to turn to him with your problems. I've got to give Matthew his tea. We didn't get any shoes, he behaved too badly in the shop.'

Henry didn't quite take in what she said whilst half registering that there was something rather odd about not allowing a baby any shoes because he behaved badly. He watched Angie turn and sweep out of the room with Matthew held like a battering ram under her arm, his unshod feet waving frantically in the air behind her, and decided that he would have to go and see Father Leatham after all.

As she spooned apple purée into Matthew's mouth and as it ran unattractively down his chin, Angie went over in her mind what she had just heard. Tamsin really was a nasty little bitch, but that should come as no surprise. What a thing to have said about her father – even if it were true which of course it couldn't be. She presumed it couldn't be – but then she began to think again about how she had always suspected Henry of finding his daughter physically attractive . . . So perhaps it was true. Angie gave an involuntary shudder. How revolting! Could Henry really be capable of that? She didn't think so, but she began to wonder. That night she moved into the spare room, telling Henry that she was feeling unwell and would rather sleep elsewhere.

198

Henry, miserable and alone in the matrimonial bed, offered up a silent Hail Mary. Father Leatham had been a comfort to him that afternoon and surprisingly *au fait* with the details of every kind of sexual abuse and aberration. Henry thought how wrong it was of people to assume, as they so often did, that a priest was of necessity an unworldly man. He had learned a lot from his confessor that day and in a way he felt envious of him as he had done not infrequently in the past. There was a man who lived in the world and yet, like Jesus Himself, was not of it.

At times it had crossed Henry's mind that he should have been a priest and yet he had always known himself to be too worldly. There had been his business acumen, the money he had made and enjoyed making, there had been his passion for Angie and there had been Annie and Tamsin. All these things seemed to have turned to ashes but he would once have found them difficult to forgo. Now, with not very much money and the threat of complete ruin hanging over his head, his thoughts turned again to the priesthood. He played with the idea that if ever anything happened to Angie, he would apply to the bishop for a special dispensation to take Holy Orders. They were short of applicants. That he knew. After all, if they were taking married Anglican clergymen, then why not him? But such thinking could lead nowhere because there was Angie, for better for worse, and there was Matthew. He couldn't face the prospect of a second annulment which he thought could probably only be acquired on the grounds of the invalidity of the first one. He offered up another silent Hail Mary and asked forgiveness for having momentarily wished his wife would die.

Annie was feeling terrible. In order not to make love to Will, she had told him that she was sickening for 'flu and then had found herself stuck with this silly lie so that she had to keep faking headaches and loss of appetite, neither of which she felt. Will was clearly hurt and somewhat puzzled by his reception. It had never been like this before and it made him feel uneasy. He instinctively felt that something was wrong but couldn't imagine what. Annie had told him about all her problems with Tamsin. Perhaps that had upset her unduly but as he had only half listened to the whole saga he didn't begin to comprehend the enormity of what had been going on. He always thought that Annie made too much fuss about her daughter anyway, and as for Henry, who was a complete idiot and a bigoted Catholic of the first order, Will just thought it incredibly funny that he, of all people, should have been accused of child abuse.

Will had gone to look in on his newspaper, he was meeting a friend for lunch and wasn't sure what time he'd be back. Annie, feeling terrible, had gone to work but as she had no classes in the afternoon, she planned to come straight home at lunch-time. She hoped to have the house to herself for a while then, to have a little time to think. Tamsin, she presumed, would be at school trying, rather late in the day, to make up for lost time.

Annie had so many things on her mind as she turned into the street on her way home. She realised she hadn't yet solved the problem of the chat line being routed into her house. Perhaps she could just unplug the telephone for a couple of days and leave it at that. More importantly, there was still Tamsin's future to worry about before she felt she could even begin to think about her own or Will's – or Walter's – or Fred's. She smiled at the thought of Fred. She opened the front door and let herself into the house and stopped suddenly, her key still in the lock. From downstairs came the sound of voices. Who the hell was in the kitchen? It sounded at first like Tamsin, but why on earth wasn't Tamsin at school after all that had happened? Perhaps Will had come back earlier than he'd intended, bringing a friend. She tiptoed to the top of the stairs leading down to the kitchen and stopped to listen.

Had the girl gone out of her mind? It was Tamsin's voice that she heard echoing theatrically and quite unnaturally from below.

' "It was the nightingale, and not the lark,/That pee-ierc'd the fee-erful hollow of thy near . . ." ' Tamsin's voice throbbed and pulsated with every kind of unimaginable emotion. ' "Believe me, love, it was the nightingale . . ." ' in a high, trilling flutter as if the speaker were about to burst into tears.

Annie ran down the stairs and opened the kitchen door to find Tamsin dressed in a black miniskirt, black tights and Doc Martens with a big brown jersey newly stolen from Will, her head thrown back, her right arm stretched out, holding a book, her left hand ludicrously clutching her breast. ' "It was the nightingale and not the lark . . ." ' Tamsin began again, then wheeled around to face her mother, dropping the book on the kitchen table as she did so.

'What on earth are you doing?' Annie wanted to know. 'I thought it was agreed that you would go to school and do some work for a change. Can't you stick to anything for five minutes?'

'But Mum, you don't know what's happened!' Tamsin flung her arms round her mother, nearly knocking her over as she did so and shouted joyously, 'It's brilliant, Mum, I'm going to be famous.'

Her mother wanted to know what on earth she was talking about.

'I've got the part – or I've nearly got the part of – Joo-liet – do you realise – Juliet – *Romeo and Juliet*.' Tamsin threw both her arms out and began to dance around the kitchen. ' "Gallop apace you fiery-footed steeds towards Phoebus' lodging . . ." '

Annie felt intensely irritated. 'Tamsin,' she said firmly, 'you'll never get anywhere if you don't stop telling these dreadful lies.'

'Lies!' Tamsin was furious. Of course she wasn't telling lies.

It took some time for Annie to be convinced that on this occasion Tamsin was indeed not telling lies. Tamsin had not been remotely interested when the casting director for *Romeo and Juliet* had come to the school, it was doubtful even that she had been aware of the event. But it so happened that she had been spotted in the corridor, enquiries had been made about her and she had now received a letter via the school inviting her to an audition, which letter she was able to show her mother.

Annie didn't know what to think. Clearly Tamsin was going to go for it. There could be no stopping her. Annie half hoped she wouldn't get the part. It would surely do her no good – and why had it cropped up now just when Tamsin had been in such trouble and had at last agreed to try to settle down?

'You do realise, don't you, that there will be hundreds of girls all dying to get the part?' Annie said. 'Don't set your heart on it – you'll probably be disappointed.'

Tamsin was infuriated by her mother's unenthusiastic reaction to her possible stardom and as she danced out of the room and bounded up the stairs to go and telephone her best friend, Susie, she momentarily forgot that what was involved was a television production and so was imagining her name in lights outside every cinema in the land. But then, she corrected herself, one thing leads to another.

Annie didn't want to stay in the house with Tamsin there and neither did she want to be in when Will got back. She really wanted Walter but he was at work where she might ring him if only Tamsin weren't around blocking the line chattering to Susie. There was another one who ought to be at school.

She put her head round the sitting-room door and called to her daughter's back, 'I'm going for a walk. See you later.'

Tamsin waved irritably in her mother's direction, nodding at the same time as if to imply that she had taken in what Annie said but that it was of no importance. 'So what do you think I ought to wear?' she asked urgently into the telephone, running her hand through her thick curls as she did so.

Annie sighed and almost slammed the door.

Outside the sun was shining and there was a definite hint of spring in the air. Annie took a deep breath and decided to make for Holland Park. There was nothing like a brisk walk to calm the nerves and clear the head.

Annie thought as she walked that in some strange way she had always loved Walter without having realised it. There was a gentleness about him and a peculiar quietness which gave her a sense of belonging. She couldn't believe that that feeling wouldn't last. She thought back over her marriage to Henry. If it hadn't been for Angie, she supposed she would still be married to Henry now. But she could no longer imagine it. It had been stultifying, as with Henry there were so many no-go areas; because of his Catholicism there were always forbidden pastures, and there were for Henry absolutes which might not even be questioned. Then there were, too, whole subjects which in Henry's eyes were best left unspoken about, and which, if touched on, produced nothing but discomfort and awkwardness. Annie was glad she was no longer married to him.

With Will things had been different – much easier,

more laid back, more *laissez-faire*, with each of them doing their own thing and going their own way. At first this had felt like a blessed relief to Annie who had relished a new-found independence and freedom. When Will was at home, he was so much more vital than Henry and this, too, had made her happy, but things, she now realised, had been changing even before Walter came on the scene. She had been lonely, she knew that now, although she had initially been unprepared to admit it, even to herself. Then she had begun to feel put upon by Will. It was as if he picked her up when it suited him only to push her away again when he'd had enough, like an empty plate at the end of a meal. She couldn't put up with a relationship like that for ever, in which she treated Will like a hero whenever he came home, with no real communication between them because she couldn't imagine his life when he was away, and he never discussed it and because he wasn't interested in hers. She knew he'd hardly taken in what she'd told him about Tamsin and Henry. She knew too – and this made her angry – that what he had taken in only made him laugh at Henry's expense.

She walked quickly through the park, so concerned with her thoughts that she didn't even realise that the birds had begun to sing and sap was rising in the trees. She vaguely noticed a woman passing with a bull terrier and a pekinese. Funny combination, she thought, but then people in parks were funny with their dogs.

Her thoughts turned from dogs to Fred. She wasn't sure that she really wanted to share her life with him. As far as she was concerned, Fred was a bit of a problem but she knew that Walter would be terribly sad if he had to go. She secretly hoped the beast would grow as quickly as possible, thus deciding his own fate. Annie did not consider marrying Walter at once. She would have to wait a while but she knew that she did want immediately to turn from Will to Walter. She needed his friendship, his love, his companionship, all of which were such a relief after what seemed to be the battlegrounds of her former relationships. He had an openness and a trustworthiness which she had never expected to find in anyone. He needed her, too. Of that she was certain and the thought of keeping him in suspense over her decision appalled her. She must tell him immediately and tonight she must tell Will that he would have to leave. She quickened her pace, glanced at a passing Bedlington and made her way out of the park to the nearest telephone box.

Walter was in his office with other people around. They were all discussing some exciting new specimens which had recently arrived from Niger.

'Walter,' Annie almost whispered, 'I'm telling Will tonight. He'll have to go. I love you.' And she rang off.

Walter looked stunned as he put the telephone down. The people in his office presumed he had had some terrible news. Perhaps someone had died. One of them asked if he was all right.

He gulped and said, 'Fine.'

Then they went on talking about fossils. They were all too absorbed in what they were doing or perhaps too embarrassed to enquire further, but they did notice that Walter suddenly seemed to have stopped concentrating on the peculiarly interesting matter in hand.

Will was looking serious. He stood in the middle of the sitting-room staring at the floor, his hands deep in his pockets. He hadn't really understood what Annie was saying, just as people sometimes block out news of death or of some terrible tragedy. He tossed his lank hair out of one eye.

'It doesn't matter,' he said. 'Don't worry. It's understandable. I leave you alone a lot. I haven't always behaved perfectly myself.' He looked up almost shyly to try to catch her reaction to what he had just said. 'I should try to stay at home more often – for longer periods. It's not fair on you.'

Annie was appalled. She would have to say it all over again, slowly. He'd be wanting to marry her next.

'Would it make it any easier for you if we were married?' he said. 'We could get married if you like . . .'

'Married if I like!' Annie was so angry at the suggestion that married she would in some way belong to Will and therefore no longer feel the need to stray, whilst he, no doubt, would continue precisely as before, that she found it quite easy now to tell him in no uncertain terms exactly what it was that she meant. Will had only just got back; it was easy now for him to say that he would spend less time abroad, but she had no reason to put any faith in that for a moment. In any case, she had made up her mind. Things had changed and the clock could never be put back.

The next day, while Annie was at work, Will packed his bags. He had said goodbye in the morning and told her he would be going to see his parents for a while. Then he thought he would probably take up his newspaper's offer of going to Georgia in a couple of weeks' time. He had told them yesterday that he couldn't go away again so soon. But things looked rather different now.

'We'll keep in touch,' they had assured each other politely and coldly. Then Annie had turned and run down the front doorsteps with a lump in her throat but without looking back.

When she came home again in the afternoon, she went up to her bedroom and wept. Will had forgotten to pack his dressing-gown. It still hung there on the end of the bed, limp and dejected.

Will had called a taxi which was standing outside

Annie's house, the meter ticking over, as he carried his bags out of the front door.

'Off on a trip then, Sir?' the driver enquired perkily, as he helped pile the luggage into the cab.

'You could say that,' Will replied drily and uninvitingly, looking at his watch as he spoke. He ran up the steps again one last time to drop his front-door keys back through the letter-box, and as he turned to come down again he spotted Sarah coming around the corner.

Oh God! He couldn't face Sarah just now. He hurried to get into the taxi before she saw him, but he was too late; she was running towards him waving her arms and calling. He had to stop and say hallo.

'Where're you off to in such a hurry?' Sarah asked breathlessly.

Will knew that Sarah was a gossip and as he looked at her, for a sort of moment he hated her; he'd certainly never loved her. But there was no point in dissembling, everyone would have to know soon.

'Annie's turned me out,' he replied bluntly. 'She's found someone else.' And he hopped into the cab. 'King's Cross station, please,' he said.

Sarah was furious and at first dumbfounded. Why hadn't Annie said anything to her? And what about Walter? He was a snake in the grass, not letting on to anyone about anything. First Isabel and now Annie. What had got into the man? She had never found him in the least bit attractive. Those two must have been desperate, she decided.

In fact Sarah was taken quite by surprise. She had just been coming to call on Annie, in the hope of finding either her or Will or both at home for a cup of coffee and a chat. She hadn't seen Will since he came back and had been feeling a little offended about that. Now, she thought, she had missed her chance. She had failed to ask Will where he was going. She would have liked to be able to get in touch with him. He'd probably be glad of her shoulder to cry on. Perhaps an old flame might be reignited, she thought. Who knows? It sometimes happens.

As she walked slowly back to her own house, Sarah's fury at being so excluded was tempered by a burgeoning feeling of satisfaction at the realisation that she was, almost certainly, the first one to know. She wondered how she could best deal with the information.

By the time she reached home she had more or less decided that the first thing she ought to do was to get hold of Walter and tell him that he should try to encourage Annie to have Will back. After all, it would be much better in the long run. Sarah herself might well console Will during the interim period, but in the end Annie could surely only be made happy by Will's return. Sarah was incapable of really thinking about what anyone else might want or need, or how they might feel. It didn't even occur to her that Walter might be in a position to know much more about what Annie felt than she was. Of course Walter would be at work so Sarah would have to wait until the evening before she could ring him and have a proper conversation. She rang Isabel instead, but she was out. Fanny and Camilla were engaged, as usual. Talking to each other no doubt. That left Patrick.

Patrick was amazed, not so much by what Sarah told him as by the fact that he had missed it all. He couldn't understand how that had happened. He'd only been out for half an hour during the morning. He'd had to pop round to the shops for a few things, but he had to admit that he wasn't at all surprised by the turn events had taken. He felt sorry for Will who was such a nice chap – with a lot of guts. It hardly seemed fair of Annie to have treated him like that while he was away, but then Patrick had always thought that Annie had a bit of a wild look about her. 'After all, she's bolted once,' he said darkly. 'I for one wouldn't want to be in Walter's shoes. I wonder if he realises what he's taken on.'

Sarah thought he'd get bored of her soon, and drop her. And then where would she be?

It wasn't until the following morning that Sarah was hit by a thunderbolt especially designed for her. Neil had come in late the night before, after she had already gone to bed and was asleep, so she had been deprived of the pleasure of telling him what had happened.

Having failed to get in touch with Walter all evening, she had gone angrily to bed quite early. She still planned to tell him that what he really ought to do was to persuade Annie to take Will back. If the worst came to the worst she might even just give him a quick ring at work.

In the morning Neil, who had hardly slept, was in a most unreceptive mood. Sarah, who was still fuming about all the injustices dealt out to her by her friends, went downstairs to lay and prepare the breakfast. She would oblige Neil to listen while he ate his toast. The breakfast was ready and she was sitting in her pink-and-white dressing-gown sipping a cup of coffee at the kitchen table but Neil was still upstairs. She could hear him, banging around. She couldn't think what he was doing or why he hadn't come down already as he was usually so punctual and always in a terrific hurry to get off to work and back to his Japanese businessmen. She was just about to go and call up to him when the door opened and he came in carrying a suitcase.

He looked awkward and very tired. Something in his demeanour communicated itself to Sarah, making her heart suddenly thud.

'What's that suitcase for?' she asked fatuously.

'I'm afraid I'm leaving,' he said. 'Isabel and I both felt

that it would be easier to go before the children came back from school . . .'

Isabel! The bitch!

'Camilla, hallo, it's Fanny.'

'Fanny! A voice from the past! How are you?'

'I'm fine. 'nd you?'

'Much the same, but it's a bit dull round here with everyone gone. As for you, you've quite forgotten us since you went and buried yourself in the Country.'

'Oh, nonsense, of course I haven't. But you know what it's like – the weeks go by and then the months – and then you realise you haven't been in touch for a while. Anyway, what's the news? You've still got Sarah. What's she up to?'

'Funnily enough, I saw her this afternoon. She's training to become a counsellor.'

'A counsellor! Sarah! I wouldn't go to her with my problems.'

'You don't realise. She's changed.'

'I should hope so. But what on earth made her think of doing that?'

'Well, when Neil left she went to this counsellor and, according to her, it was the most wonderful thing that had ever happened to her. She learned so much about herself.'

'That's good. What did she learn?'

'For one thing she learned that she was more intelligent than Neil. She also learned that she was more sensitive, more artistic and something else – something most peculiar – oh, yes, she discovered that she had to learn to express her own personality through – oh, I can't remember – anyway some kind of selfishness.'

'So having been counselled, she's learning to become a counsellor herself?'

'That's right. She can think of nothing else, but I rather think she may have lost her sense of humour.'

'I'm not sure she ever had any.'

'Come on Fanny. She used to be all right – in the good old days.'

'By the way, did you see *Romeo and Juliet*? The *Romeo and Juliet*.'

'Of course I did. You have to admit, she was pretty good.'

'Well – she was all right. India had a few comments to make.'

'So, how's India?'

'India's very well. Working hard at school. I expect you knew she got eleven straight "A"s in her GCSEs, didn't you?'

'Come on Fanny. We all knew that. But that was over a year ago. Before you left.'

'I suppose it was. But still I can't help feeling relieved that she's doing something sensible, concentrating on her work. I feel really sorry for Annie with Tamsin. I mean, it's all very well. But there you go. India says Tamsin's got another part – in some major feature film. I'd be dreadfully worried.'

'Oh, I dunno. You can't deny that she was a wonderful Juliet. I'm glad for her if she has got another part. Good luck to her.'

'Has anyone heard from Annie, in fact?'

'Not since she and Walter left, I don't think. They've gone somewhere in the West Country.'

'Yes, I knew that. Crewkerne? Honiton? Somewhere like that.'

'Oh, I can't remember where they've gone, but Walter's got this job as curator in some boring old museum.'

'That's right. Do you suppose they took the dinosaur or whatever it was with them?'

'God alone knows. Peculiar wasn't it, the way Annie fell for Walter?'

'There's nowt so queer as folk, as the saying goes.'

'True enough.'

'But do you think they're happy?'

'It seems unlikely, don't you think?'

'Well, I wouldn't want to live with Walter – after all, Sarah always said he was gay.'

'I rather think we can discount that now. I just don't know what Annie does all day, although someone said she'd gone back to what she used to do. Picture research, or something. I suppose she can do that from home. I think she comes up to London quite a bit.'

'Probably wants to escape from Walter – but then she obviously has peculiar taste. Look at Henry. Ever since Angie left, he's apparently been trying to become a priest.'

'Oh, I know. But then you see I think Angie always believed that it was true about him and Tamsin. That was why she left – not because of Lloyd's in the end.'

'I'm sure it was. But didn't you believe it – about the abuse I mean?'

'Well, perhaps. I don't know. What about you?'

'Yes, of course. I'm sure it was true.'

'Well, we'll never know. By the way, have you heard about the people who've moved into Walter's house?'

'What about them?'

'Apparently – I don't know if this is true, although I heard it on very good authority – but apparently she killed her baby.'

'Oh, Camilla, don't say such things. That can't be true.'

'I don't know. It's just what I've been told.'

'Look, I must go now, we've been talking for ages. I

really rang to say I was coming to London. Can we have lunch?'

'Of course. What fun – then I'll be able to tell you all the gossip.'

NORA NAISH

The Magistrate's Tale

Mary Chicon has never married. Her irascible old father has seen to that, keeping Mary with him on the Cotswold farm where they have lived since Mary's mother, Flora, left.

Now Mary is the new magistrate on the Frenester bench. The first woman to gain such standing, she takes her new responsibilities seriously. So when Hannah, a tearaway teenager in need of care and protection, is brought before the court, Mary offers her a foster home, a gesture which will have unforeseen consequences for Hannah, and for the household. Mary's life is further disrupted by the reappearance of her only ever suitor, David, as her mother's solicitor. Having left the past behind her, the prospects of resuming contact with Flora – and David – is a daunting one for Mary . . .

'Nora Naish's growing legion of admirers will be unable to put this book down. Once again, she wins all the tricks hands down'
Gloucester Citizen

'Nora Naish knows how to tell a good story'
Evening Standard

SALLY BRAMPTON

Lovesick

Martha's got a secret – pass it on . . .

Harry, Martha, Phil, Jane and David – artist, teacher, lawyer, interior designer and businessman. Five people, all successful and all related in one way or another – a wife, a mother, a friend, a husband, a lover.

Outwardly they are ordinary people with ordinary lives, all their worries buried deep below the surface. But when Martha leaves Harry, launching herself exuberantly on a blazing affair engineered by her sister Jane, she triggers a chain of events that will uncover the most devasting secret of all.

A bitter-sweet, contemporary novel about friendship, love – and the sometimes deadly consequences of both.

'Sally Brampton is an excellent writer'
Literary Review

MARION HALLIGAN

Wishbone

'The man opposite Emmanuelle Latimer caught her
with his glance and said, What would you wish? She
replied, without thinking, I would wish for the gift of
making dangerous choices.'

Emmanuelle Latimer appears to have it all: a beautiful
house, a successful husband, two clever children, a
lovely face. But she longs for excitement, passion and
danger . . . while her husband would like to spend
more time with his family.

The night she first wears the daring silk dress in a
seductive shade of ripe aubergine is the night her
husband has a stroke – and everything changes.
Suddenly, what the Latimers, their household, their
friends, wish for is coming true – in quite unexpected
ways.

A sparkling, witty, sharp portrait of modern
marriage.

'Her writing shimmers as much as the subject . . .
celebrating and catching life as millions have known it.'
Canberra Times

A Selected List of Fiction Available from Mandarin

☐	7493 1898 8	**Lovesick**	Sally Brampton	£5.99
☐	7493 2287 X	**The Pinprick**	Karina Cory	£5.99
☐	7493 1983 6	**The End of the Hunt**	Thomas Flanagan	£6.99
☐	7493 1319 6	**Air and Angels**	Susan Hill	£5.99
☐	7493 1518 0	**The Ex-Wives**	Deborah Moggach	£5.99
☐	7493 2014 1	**Changing Babies**	Deborah Moggach	£5.99
☐	7493 2251 9	**Acquired Tastes**	Simone Mondesir	£5.99
☐	7493 1906 2	**The Magistrate's Tale**	Nora Naish	£5.99
☐	7493 1558 X	**Sunday Lunch**	Nora Naish	£5.99
☐	7493 1559 8	**The Butterly Box**	Nora Naish	£5.99
☐	7493 2221 7	**The Jewel in the Crown**	Paul Scott	£5.99
☐	7493 1789 2	**Special Relationship**	Robyn Sisman	£5.99
☐	7493 9591 5	**Hearing Voices**	A. N. Wilson	£5.99